Riverboat Roulette

Read all the mysteries in the

NANCY DREW DIARIES

Nancy Drew

DIARIES™

Riverboat Roulette

#14

CAROLYN KEENE

Aladdin
NEW YORK   LONDON   TORONTO   SYDNEY   NEW DELHI

This book is a work of fiction. Any references to historical events, real people,
or real places are used fictitiously. Other names, characters, places, and events are products of the
author's imagination, and any resemblance to actual events or places or persons,
living or dead, is entirely coincidental.

ALADDIN

An imprint of Simon & Schuster Children's Publishing Division

1230 Avenue of the Americas, New York, NY 10020

First Aladdin paperback edition January 2017

Text copyright © 2017 by Simon & Schuster, Inc.

Cover illustration copyright © 2017 by Erin McGuire

Also available in an Aladdin hardcover edition.

All rights reserved, including the right of reproduction in whole or in part in any form.

ALADDIN and related logo are registered trademarks of Simon & Schuster, Inc.

NANCY DREW, NANCY DREW DIARIES, and related logo are
trademarks of Simon & Schuster, Inc.

For information about special discounts for bulk purchases, please contact
Simon & Schuster Special Sales at 1-866-506-1949 or business@simonandschuster.com.

The Simon & Schuster Speakers Bureau can bring authors to your live event.
For more information or to book an event contact the Simon & Schuster Speakers Bureau
at 1-866-248-3049 or visit our website at www.simonspeakers.com.

Cover designed by Karin Paprocki

Interior designed by Mike Rosamilia

The text of this book was set in Adobe Caslon Pro.

Manufactured in the United States of America 1216 OFF

2 4 6 8 10 9 7 5 3 1

Library of Congress Control Number 2016942745

ISBN 978-1-4814-6599-1 (hc)

ISBN 978-1-4814-6598-4 (pbk)

ISBN 978-1-4814-6600-4 (eBook)

Contents

Dear Diary,

EVERY YEAR GEORGE, BESS, AND I GO to the Casino Night charity gala in support of Pet Crusaders, a dog and cat rescue organization that Bess's mom is on the board for. It's always one of my favorite events of the year, and this year is extra exciting for two reasons: George is playing in the poker tournament for the first time, *and* the gala is taking place on a restored riverboat. The night took an unexpected turn, however, when a case suddenly popped up and I had to race against the clock to solve it. I can't decide if it was exciting or just stressful!

Riverboat Roulette

CHAPTER ONE

Take Me to the River

"GEORGE, YOU'VE COUNTED THAT MONEY eight times," my friend Bess Marvin said from the passenger seat of my car. "I promise, you have enough for the entry fee."

"I just want to make sure," her cousin, George Fayne, said from the backseat, where she was rifling through a large stack of twenty-dollar bills. I slowly rolled up my car window as I inched forward in rush-hour traffic. The last thing we needed was for any of George's hard-earned money to fly out the window.

Bess gave me an exasperated look. I shrugged with

a half smile. Bess knows that George gets fixated on things she's passionate about, and there are few things George is more passionate about than poker. Her dad taught her when she was five, and now she plays every weekend with her family; she even watches the World Series of Poker on TV.

Bess is very even-keeled and doesn't tend to become obsessed with things like games or new gadgets the way George does. In a lot of ways George and Bess are polar opposites, even though they're incredibly close. George would wear jeans and a T-shirt every day if she could, while Bess is a bit of a fashionista. (Take tonight, for example. Bess had spent weeks looking for the perfect dress for the charity event we were attending before picking a gorgeous asymmetrical ruby-red gown, while George wore the same black pantsuit she wears to any event that requires dressing up.) George loves technology, while Bess would rather send a paper letter than an e-mail. In general, I fall between them—for instance, I didn't buy a new dress for tonight, but I did spend a good hour going through my closet choosing which dress to wear.

When it comes to obsessive behavior, however, I'm probably closer to George. I'm an amateur detective; I solve mysteries around town, like if something goes missing or someone is being blackmailed. When I'm on a case, I can barely think about anything else.

"Okay," George announced. "It's confirmed that I have the entry fee." She carefully put the money back in her wallet.

"I can't believe how much money you were able to save," I told George. "I don't think I've ever seen that much cash in one place before."

"Well, if everything goes according to plan," Bess said, "you should see a lot more tonight. My mom told me that this event is supposed to bring in over a hundred thousand dollars."

We were headed to the annual charity Casino Night hosted by River Heights Pet Crusaders, the animal-rescue organization for which Bess's mom— and George's aunt—sat on the board. We went every year and it was always fun—getting dressed up, eating fancy food, and watching the big poker tournament. However, this was the first year we were allowed to actually *enter* the tournament, rather than just watch it. Bess and I weren't big poker players, but we were excited to support George.

"That's a lot of money for Pet Crusaders!" I said to Bess. "I hope your mom is happy."

"Yeah," Bess replied with a smile, "it's more than they've ever raised before."

"Probably because it's the first time they've gotten Brett Garner to attend," George suggested.

I saw that Bess was trying hard not to smile. "I'm not sure Brett's as big of a draw as you think he is, George."

George looked at us wide-eyed. "But Brett Garner is one of the most famous poker players in the United States. He's won the World Series of Poker twice!"

"I know he's impressive," I said. "I'm just not sure the average River Heights citizen knows who he is. Professional poker is still a pretty niche game."

"If Ned were here, he'd back me up," George grumbled. Ned Nickerson, my boyfriend, shared George's love of poker. Unfortunately, he was out of town at his cousin's wedding.

"I think the event is so popular because it's on a boat this year," I said. For the first time, the gala was being held on the *Delta Queen*, a refurbished riverboat that was originally built in the late 1800s. Back then, it had transported people up and down the river in luxury. It used to have a full restaurant; entertainment, including a casino floor; and dancing with live music. Now it just hosted short dinner cruises. It was well known in River Heights that Buddy Gibson, the owner and captain, had saved up for years to buy and restore the *Delta Queen*. His stepdad had been a riverboat captain, and Buddy had always dreamed of continuing the family tradition. It took him close to two years to get it back into working condition; there'd been a big story in the *River Heights Bugle* when it had finally opened. Tickets were notoriously hard to secure.

Bess grinned. "Mom was really proud when she

was able to rent it. Apparently, Buddy gave her a great rate." She leaned in to whisper, even though it was just the three of us in the car. "Seriously, my mom got him to let Pet Crusaders use it for almost nothing."

I smiled, then glanced over and noticed Bess clenching her fist, something I knew she did only when she was stressed out. If we were using George's poker language, it would be her "tell," or signal, that something was wrong.

"Are you nervous, Bess?" I asked.

"A little," she replied. "It's just that my mom has been working so hard on this event that I want it to go perfectly. Margot, the head of Pet Crusaders, is really high-strung. She's been flying off the handle if anything is even slightly off. The other night I saw my mom crying; Margot yelled at her because the caterers were going to switch green olives for black olives on one of the appetizers."

"I've seen Margot at the galas, but she's always rushing around, so I've never actually met her. But now

I have to meet her to tell her not to mess with my aunt," George muttered.

Bess looked up at her in alarm. "Don't say that! Margot's going about it the wrong way, but I understand why she's putting so much pressure on this event. She's going to use the money to open a second no-kill shelter in River Heights. That's twice the number of dogs and cats that will be saved every year."

George looked chagrined. "Great! Now I sound like a heartless monster."

We pulled into the parking lot, hopped out of the car, and headed to the boarding area. Well-dressed couples ambled about, slowly making their way toward the bright white boat. The light from the setting sun reflected off the vessel's surface. Each deck of the three-story riverboat looked almost like an elongated tier of a wedding cake. My favorite detail was the carved railings around each deck that from a distance looked like lace. At the front, large steam pipes proudly stood tall, and a red paddle wheel was at the boat's rear. It looked both delicate and strong.

Bess led us through the maze of cars, scanning the parking lot for her mother.

"It looks like a good turnout," I noted.

All of a sudden, a voice called out, "Bess! Over here!"

We turned to see Bess's mom waving at us and hurried over to her.

"I'm so glad you girls could make it," Mrs. Marvin said.

"We wouldn't miss it," I said.

"There's no way I would skip out on seeing Brett Garner," George said enthusiastically.

"Or any event that supports the lives of animals," I added.

"We got our cat, Joey, from Pet Crusaders, and he's the best," George agreed.

"So how's it going so far, Mom?" Bess asked.

"Oh, well, you know Margot. There was a lot of drama getting everything ready this afternoon, but once we shove off, I'm sure it will be fine."

Mrs. Marvin led us up the metal boarding ramp. I was about to hand my ticket to the usher when a tall woman with short red hair came marching toward me. Her hair was pushed back so it looked like flames coming off her head. As she tore down the ramp, her black shawl billowing behind her, she reminded me of a picture of an evil faerie I'd seen in a book of Irish mythology. I found myself taking a step back, my hands reaching instinctively for my friends.

"You," she said with a hiss, "are not allowed on this boat."

CHAPTER TWO

Mark Twain

I STARED AT THE WOMAN. MY MOUTH OPENED and closed like a fish's as I struggled to come up with a response.

"Margot," came a voice from behind me. "Be reasonable."

I turned to see a small, mousy woman with bangs and glasses standing next to a man sporting similar glasses.

"Reasonable?" Margot hissed. I realized that Margot wasn't objecting to me and my friends boarding, but the couple behind us. My shock was quickly replaced by curiosity. What did Margot have against this nice-seeming couple?

"Was it reasonable when you released mice into our cat-adoption event, making all our cats go mad chasing them around the gym?" Margot asked. Fury flew off her like beads of sweat.

"That wasn't—" the woman started to say, but Margot cut her off.

"Was it reasonable when you distributed that pamphlet that said all our cats were feral and would never be socialized enough to live in a house with children?"

"Margot!" the man said forcefully. "Joanne and I told you that we had nothing to do with either of those incidents."

"And I told you, Patrick," Margot retorted, "that I don't believe you!"

The woman sighed. "Just because we work for a different pet-rescue organization doesn't make us the enemy."

Margot cocked her eyebrow defiantly. One look

at her face showed me that there was nothing these people could say to convince her that this was true.

"My wife is right," Patrick said. "We're all on the same team; we want to save as many animals as we can."

"In any case," Joanne continued, "we bought our tickets fair and square."

"Then we'll give you a refund," Margot said icily.

Mrs. Marvin stepped forward, brushing past me to put a calming hand on Margot's shoulder. "Do you really want to give back that money?" she asked. "Think of the new shelter. Every dollar helps."

Margot turned sharply toward Mrs. Marvin, and I thought she was about to yell at her for getting involved. But before Margot had a chance to respond, a tall man with a bushy beard and a crisp white captain's uniform approached. I recognized him from photos online as Buddy Gibson.

"I've held departure as long as I can due to the traffic," he told Margot, "but we need to leave ASAP to keep our schedule."

Margot looked from Buddy to Mrs. Marvin to

Joanne. Finally she set her mouth in a straight line. "All right," she said. "You can come onboard, but if anything untoward happens in the three hours we are on this boat, I'll have the police waiting to arrest you the second we're back on dry land."

"Fine," Patrick huffed. "But our only plan is to play poker and support homeless animals."

He and Joanne marched onboard, pushing roughly past Margot, who stood watching them with a look of pure disgust on her face. After a moment she turned with a dramatic swish of her dress and followed them.

"Wow," George whispered. "Who knew there was so much drama in the world of pet rescue?"

"Haven't you learned by now?" I asked. "There's drama everywhere." In my years of sleuthing I'd investigated cases involving historical museums, ballet companies, and organic farms. I had learned that people could get heated and passionate about anything.

"Well, let's hope that was the last of the drama for tonight," Bess said.

"Yes," Mrs. Marvin agreed wholeheartedly. "Come on, girls. Let's get you all checked in and onboard."

Mrs. Marvin led us up the gangplank to a check-in desk area, with an office set up behind it. A thin woman holding a clipboard was standing there. She was pale with long, dark hair and sad eyes. Even though she grinned at us, I had a sense that her mind was a million miles away.

"This is Catherine," Mrs. Marvin said. "She is going to take care of you."

"That's an awesome watch!" George said, indicating the high-tech timepiece that Catherine was wearing.

She self-consciously pulled down the sleeve of her jacket to cover it. "I know it doesn't really go with my outfit, but I just feel better when I wear it," Catherine explained.

"That's a satellite GPS watch, right?" George asked.

"Yeah, it's incredibly precise."

"If I had a watch like that, I'd never take it off either," George said.

"Catherine is the rock of this whole operation," Mrs. Marvin said, steering us back on topic.

Catherine looked down shyly. "I'm just doing my job."

"She's gone above and beyond her job duties," Mrs. Marvin replied. "Not only is she the one who suggested we ask Buddy to let us use his beautiful boat, but she's here tonight even though her mother is in the hospital undergoing cancer treatments."

George, Bess, and I all looked at Catherine in alarm. "I'm so sorry to hear about your mother," Bess said.

"We think she's going to be all right, but it will be a long recovery." Catherine paused for a second and looked like she wanted to say more, but didn't.

"Let us know if there's anything we can do to help," Mrs. Marvin said.

"Thanks," Catherine replied with a small smile.

"Can you get these three all checked in?" Mrs. Marvin asked her. "I want to make sure everything is going according to plan in the kitchen."

"Sure," Catherine said brightly.

"All right, girls," Mrs. Marvin told us. "You're in good hands with Catherine. I'll find you later to make sure you're having a good time."

She kissed Bess on the cheek as we said good-bye.

Catherine took our names and confirmed that we were on the list. "Are any of you entering the poker tournament?" she asked.

George puffed out her chest and stepped forward with a mixture of nervousness and pride. "I am," she said, handing over the entrance fee.

Catherine carefully counted it. Even though I'd seen George count the cash three times already, I was still nervous that somehow she'd be short.

After a moment, Catherine put the money in a steel box and handed George a stack of poker chips.

"You're assigned to table five. After ninety minutes, the four players with the most chips will proceed to the final table to play with professional poker player Brett Garner."

George didn't say anything. She just stared at her chips with a goofy grin on her face.

"Thank you," Bess said to Catherine on George's behalf. "I hope your mom gets better soon."

Catherine smiled. "Your mom's been really great during all this." The way she emphasized "your mom" piqued my interest, and this time I couldn't resist.

"Has someone *not* been great with you about this?" I asked.

Catherine looked around and then said quietly, "Let's just say that Margot is amazing with animals, but not as good with people. She didn't understand why I would need extra time off to take care of my mom and help my brother."

"I'm sorry," I said. "That's tough."

"But," Catherine said, "enough about me and my problems. This night is supposed to be fun. Go have a good time!"

We thanked her for her help and entered the big room on the main deck of the boat. It was about the size of a high school gym, but much fancier! The dark mahogany walls had windows and doors to the outer deck, and the setting sun filled the room with a golden glow. A red-and-gold rug covered most of the floor, but you could still make out the edges of the hardwood floor, which matched the walls. There were eight poker tables in the center of the room, with a dance floor and stage on one end. Men and women in crisp white shirts and black vests stood at each table, ready to deal as soon as we pushed off from the shore. Chandeliers made of gold and crystal hung from the ceiling. Except for the security cameras dangling from the ceiling at opposite corners of the room, I felt transported back in time to the late nineteenth century, when traveling was as much about the journey as the destination.

I looked at George and Bess, who seemed as enchanted as I was. Then I felt the boat lurch as the engine turned on and a loud horn blasted above us.

"MARK TWAIN!" a voice blared over the loud-speaker.

"Did he just say 'Mark Twain'?" George asked. "Like the author of *Tom Sawyer* and *Huckleberry Finn*?"

"Yeah." I nodded. "I read about it online. 'Mark twain' means the water is deep enough for the boat to proceed. And it was actually a pen name. His real name was Samuel Clemens. He was a riverboat captain, so that's why he chose it."

"That's neat," George said. Then she suddenly stood up straighter. "Oh my gosh," she whispered.

"What?" Bess asked.

"There's Brett Garner." I followed where she was looking to see a young man wearing a ratty sweatshirt, wraparound sunglasses, and a beat-up baseball cap pulled low on his head.

"He could have cleaned up a little," Bess muttered. "He looks dressed for a day of lounging on the couch, not a charity gala."

"He's here," George said. "He's supporting Pet Crusaders. Who cares what he's wearing?"

George and Bess always fight about the importance of dressing the part. George thinks people should wear whatever they feel comfortable in; Bess thinks clothes are an important way of showing respect toward your environment and peers.

Before they could hash it out for the umpteenth

time, Margot stepped onto the stage. An old-fashioned safe sat on a table next to her.

"Attention, ladies and gentlemen," she said into a microphone. "Welcome to the Twenty-Third Annual Casino Night benefitting the cats and dogs of Pet Crusaders." The whole room clapped and cheered. I noticed several people holding up their phones, filming Margot as she spoke. Margot beamed at the crowd. "As many of you know, we are in the process of building a new shelter. The completion of that shelter will allow us to house twice the number of animals that we do currently. Our goal is for no cat or dog to end up in a kill shelter."

There was more clapping and cheering. Through the crowd I spied Joanne and Patrick, who were dutifully applauding but didn't look happy about it. I made a mental note to keep an eye on them throughout the evening.

"I am happy to announce," Margot continued, "that thanks to your generosity, we have raised over one hundred thousand dollars tonight!" The applause grew louder. Onstage, Margot beckoned to Catherine, who came forward carrying a large steel box. Margot carefully entered a combination into the lock on the front of the safe, then took the box from Catherine and placed it inside. Margot then closed the door with a dramatic flourish and spun the safe's large wheel, locking it.

"Let the games begin!" she said loudly.

After checking our coats, Bess and I walked George to her table, where she sat and introduced herself to the dealer and the other players. Within a few minutes, the game had started with a steady rhythm: players plunking their chips down, the slap of cards, the back-and-forth of betting and folding. George was in her element, laser-focused on her cards and the dealer's cards. Bess and I could have been abducted by aliens and she wouldn't have noticed.

My eyes wandered the room. I wasn't sure why, but *something* felt off. I don't pretend to think that I have psychic abilities, but sometimes I do get what some people would call a Spidey sense—a feeling that something is about to go wrong. I've learned over the years that it means that I've observed something but haven't consciously registered it. I read an article that said your brain processes information faster than you realize, and that's what informs our "gut reactions."

Suddenly I heard a loud crash behind me.

I whipped my head around to see a waiter, wearing a name tag that said ANDY, holding an empty tray. Joanne was standing next to him, soaking wet, as was the final poker table, where Brett, apparently still dry, was sitting.

Bess and I rushed over to Joanne, Patrick right behind us. The entire room seemed to have stopped.

"Are you okay?" Patrick asked Joanne.

"Fine," Joanne said tersely. "Just wet."

"What happened?" I asked, looking between Andy and Joanne. Andy was bright red, clearly humiliated.

"I was on my way to the restroom, when Andy here came flying into me."

"I'm so, so sorry, ma'am," Andy said in a high and

nasally voice. "I tripped." He looked at the ground. "I'm not sure on what, though."

Joanne took a deep breath, as if trying to calm herself. "It's okay," she said after a moment. "Accidents happen. I think I will go to the restroom and dry off."

Andy looked greatly relieved. "I'll find you later." He paused. "And bring you a complimentary drink, of course."

"That would be nice," Joanne said, as she headed toward the bathroom.

"I'll walk with you," Patrick said, following after her.

Andy turned to Brett. "And you, sir. Are you okay?"

"Oh, I'm fine," Brett said. "Barely a drop on me. Can't say the same for the table, though."

The green felt on the table was soaking.

"Let's see if we can get this dried off," Bess said, taking a towel from Andy.

"That's not going to work," Brett said. "You'll just tear the felt. We're going to need a new table. And new decks of cards," he said, holding up a sopping-wet playing card.

"Don't worry, sir, I'll take care of everything," Andy said. His voice had somehow gotten even higher. I could tell he was starting to panic.

I was going to offer to find help, when Brett replied with, "Hey, I can take care of getting new decks from one of the dealers. You just work on drying the table."

"I can't ask you to do that," Andy said. "You're the guest of honor!"

"I was a waiter in a past life, bro. I've been where you are. Let me help you make this right."

Andy smiled at him gratefully. "Okay, if you really don't mind . . ."

"I'm all over it," Brett reassured him.

"Do you need help with anything else?" Bess asked.

"No, no, I'm good. Thank you," Andy said adamantly. "Please just go back to enjoying the event."

Since it seemed like continuing to draw attention to Andy's accident would just stress him out more, Bess and I drifted away.

"Do you think Joanne caused the crash on purpose?" Bess asked.

I shrugged. "I don't know. That seems like it would cause more harm to her than the event."

"That's true," Bess agreed. "It's just weird, since Margot was so insistent that Joanne and Patrick were going to do something to sabotage it."

"And you guys say *I'm* always looking for a case!" I joked.

"Guess I've spent too much time hanging around you!" She laughed.

We headed back to George's table. We had watched only a few hands when a voice called out behind us. "Nancy! Bess!"

We turned around to see Mrs. Marvin rapidly approaching us. "You need to come quickly. Something terrible has happened!"

CHAPTER THREE

On the Clock

BESS AND I FOLLOWED MRS. MARVIN through the crowd. She was a woman on a mission as she artfully dodged waiters and slalomed between poker tables.

"What's going on?" I asked her when she finally stopped.

"I think it's better if Margot tells you," Mrs. Marvin replied.

I looked at Bess. She shrugged.

Mrs. Marvin led us through a door at the end of the deck. As we stepped through, we were greeted by intense heat and a painfully loud hissing noise. Immediately I threw my hands over my ears and closed my eyes. After a second, I realized that closing my eyes wasn't helping anything. I slowly opened them to see a large steam engine in the center of the room. A giant piston moved back and forth in a smooth rowing motion, which presumably made the boat's paddle wheel turn. It was fascinating to watch all the parts moving together so seamlessly—especially knowing that this particular engine had been in operation since the late 1800s. I could have stood there and watched the engine for hours, but I was distracted by Margot and Catherine in the corner.

Margot was pacing in circles. I could see her lips moving, but I couldn't hear what she was saying over the sound of the engine. Catherine, meanwhile, looked almost catatonic. She stared into space, her eyes unblinking.

"Is she okay?" Bess asked Mrs. Marvin.

At the sound of her voice, Margot stopped pacing and focused her attention on us, piercing us with her icy stare. After a long beat she approached us.

"I thought you said you were bringing help," Margot asked in a freakishly calm voice.

"Margot, this is Nancy Drew. You already know my daughter, Bess. Nancy is an accomplished detective," Mrs. Marvin said.

"I am a detective, it's true," I offered.

Margot raised her eyebrow. "This situation requires a professional. No offense, but we need someone with a little more experience than the Case of the Stolen Lollipops from Mrs. Benson's Fourth-Grade Classroom."

"Nancy has solved cases for important business owners throughout River Heights!" Bess said protectively. She hates when people make assumptions based on age, gender, or race.

"She often works with the River Heights Police Department," Mrs. Marvin added.

Margo's face shifted slightly.

"If you feel comfortable sharing what happened with me, I'd be happy to let you know if I think I could help or if it should be handled by the police," I told Margot. When someone underestimates you, I often find it best to be exceedingly polite. Hannah, our housekeeper, who has helped around our house since my mother died when I was little, always says that you catch more flies with honey than with vinegar. As with most things, I've found that she's 100 percent right.

There was another long moment as Margot held me in her gaze. I'd never met anyone with such intense eyes before. Finally she let out a sigh before blurting, "The money is gone!"

"What?" I asked, shocked.

"The money is gone," Margot repeated.

"All of it?" I asked.

Margot looked grim. "All one hundred thousand, gone."

My jaw dropped.

"But it was in the safe," Bess said.

Margot nodded. "And it was supposed to stay there until we docked. I was going to take it home and deposit it in the bank first thing tomorrow morning."

"How did you discover that it was missing?" I asked.

"Mr. Lee, who won the tournament last year, lost all his chips on an early hand. He approached Catherine and begged to be allowed to buy back in."

"I told him no," Catherine piped up from the corner.

"But," Margot continued, "I overheard and figured, why not let him? It's extra money we can put toward the new shelter. I went to add his money to the safe and discovered that all of it was gone."

She paused and took a deep breath. I realized that Margot was fighting back tears. "We're not going to be able to build the new shelter now," she said, her voice breaking as a tear rolled down her cheek. "That's fifty animals a month we won't be able to save." Now the tears were flowing freely. She had such a tough exterior that it was hard to remember that her perfectionism was driven by a deep passion to save as many animals as she could.

"I'm going to find George," Bess whispered in my ear. "We're going to need all the help we can get." I nodded and Bess slipped out of the engine room.

Mrs. Marvin stepped forward, rubbing Margot's back. "Can you help, Nancy?"

"Well," I said, "the good news is that we know that no one has gotten off the boat, so the money must still be onboard somewhere."

Margot perked up. "So you can find it?"

"I'll have to work fast," I said. "If we don't find the money before we dock, the thief will walk off the boat. Then the chances of recovering it will get much lower."

"So what do you suggest?" Margot asked.

"The most efficient approach would be to search all the guests," I began.

"That's a great idea," Catherine said eagerly.

"That's a terrible idea," Margot said at the same time.

"We would probably find the money," I said.

"The people on this boat are the Who's Who of River Heights. If I subject them to the humiliation of a search without proof that they did anything wrong, they will never give another penny to Pet Crusaders," Margot said.

"Margot's right," Mrs. Marvin interjected. "There are a lot of people here who are very important. They won't take kindly to the idea of being searched."

I nodded. "Then I think the next step is to talk to Buddy."

"Buddy has been steering the boat this entire time," Catherine said. "How can he help?"

Margot and Mrs. Marvin looked to me for an answer. I could sense Margot's faith in me fading. She'd been skeptical of a teen detective from the start, and now it seemed like I was suggesting one bad idea after another.

I took a deep breath. "I noticed security cameras in the main ballroom," I explained. "I'm sure Buddy has one pointed at the safe. If we explain what happened, I'm sure he'll let us review the footage."

"Okay," Margot agreed. "Let's go ask Buddy."

We made our way out of the engine room, and my ears immediately felt relief. Whether it was due to the pressure from the small, hot room or from Margot's interrogation, I realized that sweat had been pouring down my face.

As we made our way to the front of the boat, Bess and George approached.

"What's the plan?" George asked, jumping right into the swing of the investigation.

I explained about checking out the security cameras. "This might be your fastest case yet!" George said.

"Don't jinx it!" Bess said behind her.

"Did you have to quit your game?" I asked George. If this case was as simple as reviewing security camera footage, then it wasn't worth her abandoning her dream.

"Not yet," George said. "They're holding my place. They just put the ante in—"

"What's the ante again?" Bess interrupted.

George sighed dramatically. "I've explained this a million times," she said.

"And I've explained the difference between an empire waist and an A-line skirt a million times too, and you still get them mixed up," Bess retorted. "We all have different strengths and interests."

George nodded. "You're right. I'm sorry."

That was the thing about Bess and George. They constantly bickered, but they almost always made up within a matter of minutes.

"Anyway," George said, "the ante is basically what you put in to get your hand. The dealer will put in the ante for me and fold my hand—that means give up on the hand," she explained before Bess could ask, "on every turn. If I stay away for long enough, I'll eventually go through all my chips without playing another hand."

"We won't let that happen," I said.

"If it does, it's because the case is more important," George said. I looked at her and smiled. I'm so lucky to have friends who stand by my side no matter what.

Margot opened a door and we followed her up a set of steep stairs. Outside on the river, a cold wind blew. None of us were wearing coats. I felt my teeth start to chatter as we clanged up the stairs, our footsteps echoing on the metal. Even though we'd only pushed off forty-five minutes ago, it felt like we had traveled a long distance. The river was wide and the lights on either shore seemed far away. Inside, with the carpet, the poker tables, and the chandeliers, it was easy to forget you were actually on a journey. Out here, it felt like we were on a small boat in the middle of the wilderness.

"I really hope we have this bozo on camera," George said.

"Me too," Bess agreed. "What kind of person steals money from a charity?"

It was a good question, one I'd have to consider if the security cameras didn't have answers. I'd learned over the years that the key to solving a case was often to forget about *who* committed the crime and focus on *why*. Once you figured out a motive, the rest usually fell into place.

We finally made it to the top deck and followed Margot to what looked like a garden shed perched in the middle. Margot tried the door, but it was locked.

"Crew only!" Buddy hollered from inside. "This deck is off-limits."

"Buddy, it's Margot! We have an emergency!"

Slowly the door creaked open and Buddy peered out. Past him, I could see a young man steering the ship's helm.

"What's going on?"

"All the money we've raised has been taken from your safe," Margot told him flatly. "We need access to your security cameras."

Buddy stared at his feet and absentmindedly tugged his right ear. "But the security cameras don't work," he said.

"What!?" Margot asked. "How is that possible?"

"Yeah," George agreed. "I thought casinos were famous for having the best security in the world."

Buddy looked down sadly. "I'm selling the boat," he said.

"But buying this boat was your dream," I said, confused. "Why are you selling it so soon after you bought it?"

"Sometimes bad things happen to people you love, and you have to give up on your dreams to care for them," Buddy explained.

"I'm sorry," I said.

"Yeah, thanks," Buddy said gruffly. "Anyway, the cameras went down a few days ago. It didn't make sense to spend the money to repair them if I was just going to be selling the boat. I'm sorry. I honestly didn't think anyone would rob a charity tournament."

Margot stared at him, furious. "If we don't recover this money, I am going to sue you for every penny we lost."

"Go ahead. I have nothing left. That's why I'm selling the boat."

Margot was going to say something else, but Mrs. Marvin intervened. "We can talk about lawsuits later. Right now we need to figure out how to get the money back."

Margot took a deep breath. I could see her working hard to control her temper. "All right, Nancy," she finally said, "you're up."

"Well," I answered, "we know that the thief is someone on this boat. And that's a great start."

"Yeah," Bess agreed, "but there are still two hundred people."

I thought back to how the waiter had crashed into

Joanne. The fact that the safe had been robbed some-time around then didn't seem like a coincidence.

"You have a place to start," George said to me. "I can tell by the look on your face. You're in sorting-through-the-clues land."

"I do have an idea. The most important thing, though," I said to Margot, Mrs. Marvin, and Catherine, "is for you to act completely normal. Our big advantage is that the thief doesn't think that anyone will check the safe until we're already back in River Heights and he or she is off the boat. The culprit has no idea that we're looking for him or her."

Margot, Mrs. Marvin, and Catherine all nodded.

I turned to Buddy. "What time are we due back at the dock?"

"Ten thirty on the dot," he said.

I checked my watch. "Just under three hours," I said.

I'd never solved a case that fast before, but the dogs and cats of River Heights were counting on me!

CHAPTER FOUR

~

Money Bags

BESS, GEORGE, AND I LAGGED BEHIND the adults as we headed back toward the main deck to strategize.

"The first thing we need to do is narrow down our list of suspects," I said.

"I think we should start with Joanne and Patrick," George suggested. "Margot seemed pretty convinced that they were up to no good."

I nodded. "We'll definitely check them out. Joanne's crash with Andy, the waiter, could have been a staged distraction, but with only three hours to crack this case, I don't want to be locked into one theory. What if we spent two hours investigating Joanne and Patrick, only to find proof that they had nothing to do with it? Then we'd have only an hour to locate the real culprit."

"That makes sense," Bess agreed. "So who else are you considering?"

I scanned the room through the window before we went back in. My eyes landed on Andy serving a couple across the room.

"Well," I began, "Joanne wasn't the only one involved in the crash that caused the distraction. Andy was too."

"And," Bess added, "if Buddy is selling the boat, then Andy's job could be in danger. He might need that money."

"True," I agreed. "We'll add him to the list."

Bess started to open the door to go inside, but stopped and turned back. "You know what I don't understand?" she asked. "How did the thief know the combination to the safe?"

I shrugged. "Margot did open it in front of everyone onboard. Anyone could have seen it."

"Especially," George added, "if they filmed it on their phone. They could have zoomed in on the video afterward and easily made out the combination."

Bess sighed. "There *were* a lot of people taking videos on their phones. So much for that helping us narrow it down!"

Suddenly something else occurred to me. "One hundred thousand dollars in cash would take up a lot of space," I said.

"And it would be heavy," George noted. "Remember how Catherine struggled to carry the box over to the safe?"

"Whoever stole it is going to need a way to get it off the boat without attracting a lot of attention," I said. "You can't just stick it in your pocket or your purse."

"So they'd need a big bag?" Bess asked.

"Yeah," I answered. "I think we need to check the coatroom for bags large enough to carry the money off the boat."

"Good idea," Bess said.

"George," I said, "go back to your game."

"Are you sure?" George asked. "Poker isn't more important than this case."

"I need you to keep your eyes on our suspects and let me know if any of them are acting suspicious while Bess and I check out the coatroom."

"Got it," George said.

Bess looked over at me, her hand on the door handle. I gave her a small nod. She pushed open the door and we strode back into the warmth of the main deck.

The gala was in full swing. All around us, players were at poker tables and roulette wheels, or on the dance floor. The general hum of two hundred people was punctuated by occasional cries of triumph or despair, depending on the luck of the draw. In the corner, I spotted Margot chatting up a man in a tuxedo. Her face looked drawn and tight, but otherwise she seemed to be doing a good job of pretending nothing was wrong. She raised one eyebrow slightly and I nodded, trying my best to reassure her that I had this under control.

Bess gave George an encouraging pat on the shoulder. "Go get 'em!"

George nodded. "You too."

She headed to her table, and Bess and I continued toward the stairs on the other side of the boat. Those led to the coatroom.

I turned to Bess. "We're going to have to get past the coat clerk. Let's use the trick we used on the Winchester case."

Bess wrinkled her nose and then nodded. "Only for you, Nancy."

She slowed her pace, giving me the lead, and turned toward the bar. When you work enough cases with your friends, they get to know all your ploys—whether they like them or not!

I headed down the stairs and walked along the hallway toward a bored young woman who was sitting behind the coat check, sipping on a soft drink and thumbing through a magazine.

"Hi!" I said brightly.

The woman reluctantly looked up.

"I am such a dummy!" I said. "I went to buy a soda and realized I left my wallet in my coat pocket."

"Do you have your coat tag?" she asked in a monotone.

I dramatically patted my pockets, turning them inside out, pretending I was looking for my tag. I then moved on to my purse, emptying the contents onto the counter in front of the clerk. No tag.

"I can't believe this!" I said frantically. "I can't find it!" Even though I had a tag from when we'd all checked our coats—and knew exactly where it was— my act was just the first part of the plan.

The woman looked completely unimpressed. "No tag, no coat," she said.

"This is a nightmare. I think it was number twenty-three, something like that? Could you go check for me, maybe?"

Before the clerk could respond, Bess came running around the corner. There was a brown wet spot on the shoulder of her dress. "Excuse me, excuse me, excuse me," she said urgently. "Is there a lost and found? I am having an emergency and I need help."

"Um, yeah, it's down the hall—"

"Great! Can you take me to it?" Bess asked. "I spilled something on my dress, and I cannot walk around like this. It's *too* embarrassing."

"Um, well, I don't think there's a dress in the lost and found," the clerk said.

"All I need is a scarf or a sweater. Anything to cover this up." Bess spied the fashion magazine on the counter. "You obviously appreciate fashion. Maybe you can help me pick something out."

The clerk perked up, pleased that Bess had noticed her interest in clothing. I would congratulate Bess later on her ability to improvise. She's a planner; when she first started helping me with cases, the going-with-the-flow aspect of investigating could trip her up, but she was handling this like a professional.

The clerk looked between me and Bess, clearly torn. Now it was my turn to jump in.

"Go help her. She is having a true emergency. I can just go back and grab my coat. Don't worry about me," I said as I pushed back behind the counter.

"You can't—" the clerk started, but Bess grabbed her by the hand, pulling her down the hall.

"Thank you so much for helping me," Bess said.

As they disappeared down the hallway, I fought my way through the coats. It was like a forest of outerwear, and most of it was black. I searched the shelves in the back, but there were very few bags. All the women had kept their purses with them. I saw a few briefcases, but none of them were big enough to hold all the money that had been stolen. I sighed. I felt bad that Bess had gotten her dress wet for no reason.

As I turned back toward the entrance, I tripped over an umbrella that had fallen down. I fell forward, grabbing fruitlessly at the row of coats in front of me. I tumbled straight through them, knocking several off their hangers.

Down the hall, I heard Bess talking to the clerk.

"Are you sure this is the best one? Maybe I should go back and take the orange cardigan."

"The orange cardigan was hideous," the clerk said. "Trust me. This was the best of the bunch."

I quickly scrambled to put the coats back on the hangers. As I worked, an envelope from a coat pocket fell onto the floor. As I picked it up, a letter fell out of the envelope. It was addressed to Brett Garner and was printed on Poker All-Stars stationery.

> *Dear Mr. Garner,*
> *This is to officially inform you that*
> *due to your poor performance in*
> *recent tournaments, we are forced to*
> *terminate our sponsorship. It is no*
> *longer possible for Poker All-Stars to*
> *pay your travel and entry fees.*
>
> *Sincerely,*
> *Jason Olsen*
> *President, Poker All-Stars*

"Thank you so much for all your help," I heard Bess say from just a few feet away.

Quickly, I shoved the letter into my pocket, grabbed my wallet out of my purse, and charged toward the exit.

"Found it," I said, just as Bess and the clerk stopped in front of the entrance to the coatroom. "Thank you."

We hightailed it down the hall. I could feel the clerk's eyes on us, but I resisted any urge to look back.

"Find anything?" Bess asked, as we rounded the corner.

"No big bags, but I did find this," I said, handing her the letter.

Bess read it as we reentered the main deck. "You think Brett might be a suspect?" she asked.

"I don't want to, but if Brett's losing his sponsorship, he's going to need money fast. That's a motive."

"Yeah, but he was across the room from the safe, right next to Andy and Joanne, during the crash. How could he have taken the money?"

"He could have tripped Andy to cause the distraction and an accomplice could have stolen the money. Beside, Bess, look!" I pointed toward Brett's chair.

Bess followed my finger to see that under Brett's seat was a huge hiking backpack—one definitely large enough to hold one hundred thousand dollars!

CHAPTER FIVE

～❦～

In the Belly of the Boat

"WE NEED TO PEEK INSIDE THAT BAG," I said.

"Absolutely," Bess agreed. "What trick are we going with this time?"

I was running through a list of my go-to schemes when I noticed George beckoning from her table. We made our way over to her.

"Nice job, George," I said, indicating the stack of chips in front of her. It was definitely the biggest pile on the table.

"I've been trying to reach you for, like, three

minutes," she said, throwing a chip into the center of the table. It was her ante, I realized.

I laughed to myself. Only George would think of three minutes as a long time. Any kind of waiting is torture for her.

The dealer finished shuffling and dealt two cards to each player. George smoothly peeked at the cards. She had a pair of fours. I recalled from George's and Ned's lessons that this was a so-so hand. She had a pair, but they were low cards. Anyone who had a pair of cards that were at all higher would beat her. It would come down to whether another four was flipped over in the shared cards. It was, I thought, definitely worth staying in the hand to find out.

"Why didn't you text us?" Bess asked.

"No service out here on the river," George said, waving her phone around dramatically. "All the trees on the riverbank probably interfere with the signal. Vegetation is really bad for cell service."

"No service? How are you holding up? Are you feeling ill?" I asked, putting my hand on her forehead.

The dealer shot me a dirty look. Talking to players during an active hand is pretty frowned upon. If this were a tournament where people were actually playing for money and not charity, there'd be no way he'd tolerate it.

George squirmed away from me. "Very funny. I can live without my phone just fine, thank you very much."

Bess and I burst out laughing. We all knew that wasn't true. A while ago we'd gone camping out by Mystic Lake, a few hours from River Heights. None of us had realized that there was no cell service there. After about three hours, George was grumpy and irritable. We couldn't figure out what was wrong with her, until Bess realized that it was the longest George had gone without being online in at least two years. As soon as cell service returned, happy George returned.

The dealer turned to George. Without a word, George threw in a ten-dollar chip as her bet. I was impressed. This was her first time playing with strangers, and she looked like a pro. I knew she'd been nervous that she would embarrass herself by not knowing some of the game's unspoken rules, but she seemed to blend right in. The dealer went around the table, asking each person if they were going to call—meaning match George's bet—or fold. One man folded; two others called.

I scanned the room, and all of a sudden, it hit me. Someone was missing.

"George, where's Joanne?" I whispered.

"That's what I wanted to tell you!" George hissed back.

"I raise," said a man across the table. He pushed in a twenty-dollar chip. The dealer turned back to George. She had to decide if she was going to match his bet, raise it, or fold. Some people play very aggressively, almost always betting over their hands. George, however, is a very logical person, and she plays a very logical way. She bets what she thinks her cards are worth and very rarely bluffs.

I knew there was no use talking to her until she had made her decision.

After what seemed like forever, but was probably

only a few seconds, George called the bet, throwing in another ten-dollar chip so that the total bet from each player was twenty dollars.

"Where's Joanne, George?" I asked the second the chip left her hand.

"A few minutes ago Andy came over to her and whispered something in her ear. Suddenly she got up and followed him across the room. It all seemed urgent and very hush-hush."

The dealer flipped the first three center cards over. No fours, which didn't help George at all.

"Where did they go?" I asked.

"All I saw was that they went through that door over there." She pointed across the ship to a door marked RESTRICTED. CREW ONLY.

This could be a clue that Andy and Joanne were working together. If I was lucky, maybe they were doing something with the money right now. If I caught them in the act, then the case would be solved with plenty of time to spare.

But what about Brett? He was a solid lead too.

And I'd already been on this case for thirty minutes—one-sixth of my total allotted time. I didn't have time to waste pursuing the wrong clue.

I took a deep breath, closed my eyes, and counted to ten. I tried to clear all thoughts from my head. It was a trick my dad had taught me. As a lawyer, he has to make tough decisions all the time, decisions that could determine whether an innocent person was put in jail or a guilty one got to walk away. He's told me that during moments when you feel under pressure, the best thing to do is pause. There's almost nothing that can't wait for a count of ten, and this way you can listen to your gut. My dad says that most often your first instinct is the correct one; it's overthinking that gets people into trouble.

By the time I got to ten, I knew what we needed to do.

"Okay," I said to Bess. "I'm going to look for Joanne and Andy. You work your magic with Brett. See if you can get him to show you inside his backpack."

"I can do that," Bess said with a grin. Bess is a

people person; aside from being a good listener and generally compassionate, she's also good at convincing others to do what she wants. She's gotten herself out of so many library late fees and parking tickets that we call it her superpower.

I charged across the room to the CREW ONLY door and, after a quick look around to make sure no one was watching, tried the doorknob. I wasn't expecting it to be open, but to my surprise, the handle turned. A lucky break! As soon as I stepped through the door, it was clear that Buddy had never intended for passengers to see this part of the boat. For as luxurious as the main deck was, this room was cold, dark, and industrial. To my left were doors that led into the kitchen. I could hear the clanging of pots and tense, agitated voices barking orders. To my right was a long, dark staircase.

I couldn't be sure that Andy had taken Joanne down the stairs rather than into the kitchen, but it was a gamble I was going to have to take. I started down the stairs. I wanted to use my cell phone to light the way, but I didn't want to tip Andy and Joanne off that

I was coming. I walked as quietly as I could, painfully aware every time my step echoed off the metal stairs.

When I got to the bottom of the steps, I was in a long hallway that stretched in both directions. In front of me a porthole revealed that we were about even with the water level. I realized that if my head was at the same level as the porthole, then my feet were underwater. I could make out murmured voices coming from my right.

Slowly, creeping along the side of the boat to make sure I didn't trip over anything, I made my way toward the voices. I could hear the water sloshing with every turn of the paddle wheel.

Ahead of me I could see moving lights—probably flashlights—in an open doorway. As I crept closer, someone shut the door from inside.

Suddenly I heard a loud *thud*. Was it the bag of money? I pressed my ear against the door. It was thick with a tight seal to keep water out in the case of a leak, so I really had to push right up against it to hear anything.

"Okay, that's enough," a man's voice said. It was muffled, but I recognized the high, nasal pitch as Andy's.

"I just need to do one more thing," a woman's voice said. I couldn't prove that it was Joanne's, but since George said she had left with Andy, I was pretty sure it was her.

"We really should be getting back. The other waiters are going to notice I'm gone."

"Hold your horses. I'll be done in a minute. Remember, I paid you for this!" There was a scraping sound as the woman grunted. It sounded like the noise I made when I'd helped Ned move into his dorm at school and had accidentally picked up the box that had his free weights in it.

What were they doing in there? I wished there was a keyhole or something I could see through. There was only so much I could deduce from their muffled voices.

"Okay, I'm done," the woman said suddenly.

"Finally," Andy said. "Let's get out of here!"

I scrambled away from the door and looked around

frantically for a place to hide. To my right, fifty feet in the direction I'd come from, I saw a bank of metal cabinets that I hadn't noticed earlier. It was my best bet. The only question was whether I could make it there in time. I ran forward, staying light on my feet to make as little noise as possible. I was glad I'd worn rubber-soled flats as opposed to the heels that Bess had encouraged me to wear. I made it to the nearest cabinet and yanked it open.

Behind me I heard the creak of a door opening. At any second, Andy's and Joanna's flashlights would catch my feet in their beams!

CHAPTER SIX

❦

A Gamble

I SLIPPED INSIDE THE CABINET AND PULLED the door closed without latching it; I couldn't risk making any noise. It was cramped inside. My head was resting against something cylindrical and metallic, and some kind of thick material was scrunched under my side. Whatever it was smelled rubbery, and when I examined it, I noticed it had what seemed to be arms and legs protruding from it. I was pretty sure it was a wet suit, but I didn't have time to examine it closely.

The only light came from the flashlight beams that shined through the crack in the cabinet door. Joanne and Andy were just inches away from me. I scrunched my eyes closed as their steps grew louder. They were right in front of me now.

Then one set of footsteps stopped abruptly. "Hold on a second," Joanne said.

"No way!" Andy said. "I need to get back. I held up my end of the deal!"

"My dress is stuck on something!" Joanne exclaimed.

I opened my eyes. I could see through the crack in the door that Joanna's dress had snagged on the corner of the cabinet.

"What?" Andy said.

"My dress is caught. If I move, it will tear. I can't bend over in these heels. Can you free it for me?"

Andy sighed. "Fine. But shine your flashlight down there so I can see."

Joanna did so, and Andy leaned down, just millimeters away from me. If he looked closely into the slightly ajar cabinet door, he would see me hiding. I held my breath.

"Be careful," Joanne said. "I borrowed this dress! I have to give it back to my friend tomorrow in mint condition."

"I'm being careful," Andy grumbled.

I was desperate to take a breath. I could feel my lungs starting to burn. When I was taking swimming lessons, the instructor made us hold our breath for as long as we could. My record was seventy-three seconds. By my estimate, I had currently been holding it for forty seconds, so I knew I could keep going, but that didn't mean it was going to be pleasant.

Finally Andy got the dress free. "There," he said. "All set."

"Thanks," Joanne said.

Andy stood up and the two of them started walking again. As slowly as I could, I let out the breath I'd been holding. When I heard their footsteps on the stairs, I considered the coast clear.

I quickly opened the cabinet door. As I did so, I knocked over the metal cylinder my head had been pushed against. When I examined it more closely, I saw that it was an oxygen tank. I pulled out the material that I had been on top of and confirmed that it was a wet suit. An oxygen tank and a wet suit?

I fished my phone from my purse and turned on the flashlight. There was a logo on the oxygen tank that read DEEP SEA ADVENTURES. That seemed odd. I knew this was a boat, but I hadn't heard of anyone going scuba diving in the river. From what I understood, the water was so murky that you couldn't see much. After a moment, I shook my head. *One mystery at a time,* I told myself. *Find the money, and then you can figure out why there's scuba gear on the boat.*

I stood up and made my way to the room Andy and Joanne had been in earlier.

I tried the handle. The door was extremely heavy, but it was unlocked. I was simultaneously relieved and disappointed. On the one hand, I was glad something was easy, but would they really leave one hundred thousand dollars in an unlocked room?

I entered the room, which seemed to be a storage area. There was stuff everywhere. This wouldn't be a bad place to hide a bag of money, and Andy could probably sneak it off after we docked under the guise of unloading supplies.

I searched the room as quickly as I could. No money. What were Joanne and Andy doing in here? Something wasn't adding up, and I could feel myself going in circles. I needed to get back to the main floor and talk this over with Bess and George.

A few minutes later, I was pushing open the door to the main deck. I checked my watch. I'd only been belowdecks for twenty minutes, but it felt like a lot longer. Bess spotted me, and as soon as I saw her face, I knew my makeup must have run while I was sweating in the cabinet. Not to mention the static electricity that had built up in my hair. Oh well. No one ever said being a detective was glamorous!

She pointed toward the ladies' room, and I met her in there. As soon as I stepped in, Bess locked the door so we could talk without interruption.

"What happened?"

I quickly gave her a recap while Bess applied powder to my face from a compact she had in her purse.

"Do you think they have the money?" she asked.

"I don't know," I said. "They're up to something, but I can't prove that it has anything to do with the money."

Bess handed me a hairbrush that she'd produced from her purse. "Smooth out that hair," she said.

"What about you?" I asked. "Did you get a look inside his bag?"

Bess's face fell. "That man is impossible," she said. "I tried every trick in the book. I complimented the bag. I told him I had been looking for a backpack like that for ages. I asked him what material it was made of. When he didn't know, I asked if I could feel it. He didn't go for anything!"

I processed what Bess had just said. "You didn't even get a peek at the bag?" I asked.

"I never got closer than one foot! He never even changed his expression. He really is a professional poker player." Bess took a step back and appraised my face, giving a small, satisfied nod. "I couldn't even tell if he was mad that I was asking about the bag. He just kept politely saying no. I felt like an annoying gnat!"

I could relate. Bess and I were in a similar situation. I knew there was something up with Joanne and Andy, just as she knew there was something suspicious in Brett's bag. But we couldn't prove that either suspect had anything to do with the missing money.

"Maybe you've lost your superpower," I said.

"Hey," Bess protested. "Even Superman has a weakness."

I grinned. "I wish George were here to hear you say that."

Just then there was a knock on the door. Bess and I looked at each other. We needed to hurry up. But then there was another knock, and another, followed by two short raps. It was our secret knock.

Bess opened the door to find George standing outside, and hustled her in.

"Did I hear you two talking about Superman?" George asked.

"Brett Garner is Bess's archenemy, her Lex Luthor," I explained.

"Well," George said, "I hope he's not my Lex Luthor, because . . . I'm officially playing him at the final table!"

"What!?" Bess and I shrieked simultaneously.

"Yeah," George said. "They called time and then they went around the room and picked the four people with the most chips, and I was one of them!"

Bess and I immediately enveloped George in a group hug. She tried to squirm out of it, but we wouldn't let her.

"Oh my gosh," Bess said. "That's amazing!"

"Joanne made it too."

"How?" I asked. "Joanne was barely at the table. She was downstairs with Andy."

"Patrick had the second most chips, but he said he was going to let Joanne play the actual final," George said.

"Is that allowed?" I asked.

George shrugged. "I mean, obviously, it wouldn't

be if this was a professional tournament, but since this is for charity, the rules are much looser. This tournament is just about having fun."

"That makes sense," Bess said.

"I'm so happy for you," I told George. "You worked hard to save up the money to enter this tournament. You really earned this!"

"You guys are going to make me cry," George said. "And you know how I feel about that!" George does her best not to express her emotions, but really she's a giant softy. I've spotted her crying at a few sappy romantic movies. "What about the case?" she asked, deflecting our attention away from her.

I sighed. "Bad news," I said. "Brett is officially a suspect."

"Nancy, that's crazy!" George said. "Brett is a hugely successful poker player. Why would he steal money from a charity?"

Bess and I quickly caught her up on the letter and the bag. George didn't say anything for a moment. She looked shell-shocked.

"Well," she finally said. "I think you're wrong, but I know the rule. We investigate all possible suspects."

"The problem now is that we have two solid leads, but no conclusive proof," I said.

There was a knock on the door. "This isn't supposed to be locked," a woman said from the outside. We couldn't stay holed up in here forever.

"Ordinarily," I said, "I would pick my top suspect and investigate them until I found evidence proving or disproving their guilt, then move on to the next best suspect. But we only have two hours left. We need to investigate both suspects at the same time."

"How?" Bess asked.

"I'm not sure," I said.

There was another knock on the door. "Seriously!" a woman outside yelled. "Open the door!"

"Just a minute!" Bess said. "My friend's not feeling well."

There was grumbling from outside.

"We need to come up with something quickly," Bess said.

"I know a way," George said quietly.

Bess and I turned to her.

"You take my spot, Nancy."

"What?" I asked.

"Take my spot at the final table," George repeated.

~❧~

CHAPTER SEVEN

All In

"GEORGE, NO," I SAID. "YOU'VE WORKED too hard for this."

"But this way you'll be able to talk to the players. You're better at questioning suspects than I am. Finding the money is more important," George said. "You remember what Joey looked like when we adopted him!"

I nodded. George's cat had been picked up by River Heights Animal Control howling under a porch during a snowstorm. He was all skin and bones, fighting off a respiratory infection, and he'd even had frostbite on his left ear.

"If Pet Crusaders hadn't rescued him from the pound, given him antibiotics, and tipped his ear, he would have died," George said. She wiped her eyes. Bess handed her a tissue. "My life would be way worse without Joey."

There was another knock on the bathroom door. "Whoever is in there, you need to unlock this door right now," a woman bellowed from outside.

"That's Margot," Bess said. "We have to go."

Bess unlocked the door to reveal Margot standing with another woman. Margot's face transformed from furious to hopeful as soon as we opened the door. I knew she wanted to ask about the case, but we couldn't risk discussing it in front of a stranger.

I shook my head subtly. I didn't want Margot to get her hopes up.

Her face fell.

I turned to George as we walked back to the main room. "Prep me for this game," I said. "I need to stay in as long as possible, so I have as much time as I can to probe Joanne and Brett about the money."

"You're playing one of the most popular poker games," George told me, "Texas Hold-'em. It's the version we usually play with Ned. Every player is dealt two cards, and then the dealer turns over five communal cards in the middle of the table. Whoever has the five best cards between their own personal cards and the communal cards wins."

"I remember," I said.

"Do you remember the order of hands?" George asked.

"I think so," I said. We quickly ran through the hands, from a pair all the way to a royal flush—a ten, jack, queen, king, and ace all in the same suit. I was pretty proud of myself for remembering all the hands, except for a full house, which George had to remind me meant a pair of two cards and three of a kind of another (like a pair of fours and three tens).

"Perfect." We'd arrived at George's table, where she picked up her chips, and then headed toward the final table. "The best way to stay in the game as long as possible is to play cautiously. If the two cards the dealer gives you aren't a pair or two high cards, like an ace and a king, then fold."

"Okay." I nodded.

"Don't bet big unless you see the potential for a fantastic hand, like a pair of aces or kings. If you do have those cards, though, you *have* to bet big. It's the only way you'll build up enough of a stack to keep going when you're deep into the game."

"Got it," I said. We were just a few feet from the final table now. All but two of the seats were filled. Brett and Joanne were seated already, as was Caleb Rainey, the owner of the local outdoor goods store, wearing his signature cowboy hat. One of the empty seats was next to Brett and the other was across the table from him. I glanced under his chair. The backpack was still there. I wanted that seat next to him. The proximity would be helpful to get a peek inside the backpack. I looked up and saw Carla Huerta, who went to school with Ned, walking toward the table. I picked up my pace, Bess and George following behind.

"The most important thing to remember," George said, "is that you should use the first few hands to get to know the other players. You'll be good at that. Try to figure out when they're bluffing and when they have legitimately good hands."

I nodded, wishing I'd taken George and Ned up on their offers to play poker more frequently. That's the thing about being a detective: you never know when a skill is going to come in handy. All I could do was my best.

Carla beat me to the table and took the seat next to Brett. I looked at my watch. There were just under two hours until we docked.

With nothing else to do, I took the last remaining seat, across from Brett and Joanne.

George clapped me on the back. "You'll do great," she said. "I've always said you had the potential to be a fantastic poker player."

"Remember, Nancy," Bess whispered into my ear, "you don't have to win. You just have to stay in until you get the information you need." I looked at her gratefully. Once again Bess had known instinctively how I was feeling and what to say.

Bess and George retreated to where the rest of the crowd was standing. I saw Mrs. Marvin and Catherine join them. Catherine looked distracted and fidgety.

I glanced around the table, paying close attention to Joanne and Brett. Joanne looked completely relaxed, almost smug. With his sunglasses on, it was hard to tell where Brett was looking, but it felt like he was staring right at me. I felt a shiver go down my back as adrenaline coursed through my veins.

"All right," the dealer said. "My name is Robert. Congratulations on making the final table of this year's Pet Crusaders Charity Poker Tournament. The four of you get to test your skills against the one and only Brett Garner. Are you ready to get started?"

All five of us nodded. This time I knew for sure that Brett was staring straight at me.

We put in our antes and Robert dealt the cards. I had a jack of spades and a two of hearts. I folded. Most of us did. Only Carla and Brett stayed in the hand, and

Brett ended up winning with two pair. As he swept up his chips, I once again felt his eyes on me.

The next hand, I drew a pair of tens. Not amazing, but enough to see the flop—what we called the dealer turning over the first three communal cards. To my utter delight, a ten was turned over. It took all my effort to not break into a grin as soon as I saw it. I raised my bet.

Joanne matched me, twirling her hair. I studied her face. She was giving nothing away. Mr. Rainey also called.

"I fold," Carla said, pushing her cards toward the dealer.

"Me too," Brett said.

Robert flipped the next card—the turn. A two of clubs.

Robert turned to me. "What would you like to do, Nancy? You can bet or check."

"I bet twenty dollars," I said, putting the appropriate chip into the pot.

"Too rich for my blood," Mr. Rainey said, setting his cards down.

"I'll see where this is going," Joanne said, twirling her hair. The only read I could get off her face was that she seemed very relaxed. Either she had nothing to do with stealing the money or she was confident in her ability to get away with the crime. The problem was I didn't know her well enough to be able to tell how she acted in stressful situations.

Robert flipped the last card over, a jack of diamonds. The hand was over. I showed my three of a kind. Joanne flipped over her cards, revealing that all she held was an ace, a very weak hand. She had been bluffing. I thought back through the hand, trying to recall if she had any kind of nervous tic or gesture. If she had a tell when she bluffed, it was possible she had a tell when she lied in real life, which could be helpful to the case. As I took my newly won chips, I remembered that she had twirled her hair. Maybe that was her tell! I needed to find out.

"Isn't this boat absolutely beautiful?" I asked.

"Gorgeous," Joanne agreed.

"I am so in love with it. I wish we could really see

all of it, not just the room where the tournament is being held." Joanne looked at me and nodded vaguely, but didn't reveal anything else. I leaned forward conspiratorally. "Did I see you go through the restricted door earlier?" I whispered.

Joanne looked at me with a perfectly neutral expression on her face. "Nope," she said. Then she twirled her hair. "Not me."

I had her tell! And it wasn't only a tell when she bluffed in poker. She also twirled her hair when she was lying in real life. Finally, some information I could use.

"Oh, sorry," I said, leaning back. "I must have seen someone who looked like you."

Robert dealt the next hand, and we were onto another round of betting, calling, raising, and folding.

The game continued this way. I was dealt a lot of bad hands that I folded right away, but every once in a while I got a good enough hand to win some chips back. It reminded me that poker had a lot of boring moments for all its exciting ones. There was an easy chatter around the game. When we'd played with George and her family, of course, we'd all talked, but I'd been surprised when I had watched a professional tournament with Ned how much the players talked to one another. Brett, however, didn't say a word. He just quietly dominated the game. His stack of chips was far and away the largest on the table. Even through his sunglasses, however, I could feel that his attention was focused on me. It was unnerving. Joanne never betrayed emotion one way or the other. She could win a huge hand or lose one and her expression didn't change. Hers was a professional-level poker face.

Before I realized it, another half hour had gone by. While I was doing okay in the game, I wasn't getting anywhere with the case.

Robert dealt another hand. I folded. Brett stayed in. When no one was looking, I moved my hand, knocking a pile of chips onto the floor.

"Oh my gosh!" I said. "I am such a klutz!"

I slid out of my chair and under the table, ostensibly picking up my chips. Brett's backpack was just two feet away from me. I crawled forward and put my hand out to open the bag's clasp, but something stopped me. I looked up to see Brett peering under the table.

I jolted up, hitting my head on the table.

"Ow! You scared me," I said.

"Find all your chips?" Brett asked.

"Just one more," I answered. I reached behind the backpack and, using a sleight of hand trick, pulled out a chip and showed it to Brett.

I returned to my seat, rubbing the back of my head. George and Bess looked at me, their eyes wide.

The game continued. I wasn't getting any good cards, and my stack of chips was decreasing with each ante. If I didn't win soon, I would be out of this game. I felt like I was letting George down by not making more progress.

"After this hand, we'll take a stretch break," Robert announced.

Suddenly it hit me. I wasn't just playing the game safe; I was playing the case safe. The time constraint had made me so rattled that I had lost my confidence.

I needed to push Joanne and Brett a lot harder. If I wanted to catch Joanne in a lie, I was going to need to be direct with her, to force her hand.

I turned to Joanne. "You were behind me on the gangplank! Did I see you get into a bit of a squabble with Margot when you got on the boat?"

Joanne looked at me sharply. "It was just a professional disagreement," she said calmly.

"Oh," I replied.

I looked at the cards Robert had dealt me: a ten and a queen, both spades.

Mr. Rainey started the bidding at two hundred dollars. I called. It wasn't a great hand, but I needed to be aggressive. Across from me Joanne raised the bet to three hundred. I looked at my stack of chips. Three hundred dollars was a good chunk of what I had left, but it was time to take a risk. I added a hundred dollars and matched her bet; so did Mr. Rainey. Brett and Carla folded.

"I mean," I said to Joanne, "I understand why Margot was suspicious. If you run your own pet-rescue organization, why are you here?"

Joanne paused and twirled her hair. "I just want to support a fellow animal rescuer."

I knew she was lying, but I didn't know about what, exactly.

Robert turned over the flop. There was jack of spades and a king of spades, as well as a seven of clubs. I looked from the flop to my hand and back. I was very, very close to having a royal flush: the best hand in all of poker. I just needed an ace of spades.

I looked down at my stack and pushed half the chips forward, my heart racing. "I'll bet five hundred dollars," I said.

"Woo-ee," Mr. Rainey said. "I'm out." He slapped down his cards.

Joanne stared at me as she pushed in five hundred dollars' worth of chips. It was a much smaller percentage of her stack than mine.

Robert flipped over the next card—the turn. It was a three of clubs. Not helpful to me at all.

"I check," I said. I turned to Joanne and decided to see how she'd respond to a more direct approach. "It's just that I thought I heard Critter Kings was in financial trouble." Of course I didn't know whether this was true, but if it was, it would be a motive for the theft. I'd watch her reaction carefully. "I know what you're trying to do," Joanne said. "You're trying to get inside my head in order to win this game. It's not going to work. I bet another five hundred dollars."

I looked from my stack of chips to Joanne's. Calling her bet would put me all in. If I lost the bet, my access to Brett and Joanne would be much more difficult. Both of them were doing well, so they would be involved in this game for a while longer. And Robert was keeping a way closer watch on outsiders talking to players than George's dealer had, so there was no chance of talking to them if I was out of the game. But I was down enough chips that if I didn't go all in now, I'd be forced to next time . . . and who knew what cards I'd have then? If I won, then at least I'd have another opportunity to question Joanne and to try to get into Brett's bag.

Slowly, I pushed my entire stack of chips into the center of the table. "I'm all in."

Behind me, I heard the crowd gasp. I looked back at George and Bess. George nodded at me. Robert looked between me and Joanne, his hand ready to flip the last card.

I held my breath as he turned it over. I just hoped I could stay in the game.

CHAPTER EIGHT

~

The River Card

IT WAS AN ACE OF SPADES! I COULDN'T believe it. I had my royal flush!

I looked across the table. Joanne's face was calm and collected. I had no idea how good her hand was, but I knew it couldn't be better than mine. I could feel the corners of my mouth twitching as I tried to fight off a smile and maintain my poker face. Winning this hand was fun, but it wasn't the point.

Joanne waited for me to reveal my cards.

"I don't think I heard your answer before," I said, as

I put down my ten of spades. "Is Kitty Kings in financial trouble?"

Joanne didn't say anything. She just stared as I pushed the jack of spades from the communal cards into a row with my ten.

"No way," I heard George say behind me. A gasp worked its way through the crowd as they realized my hand.

Joanne remained quiet, though. I left a spot for the queen I was holding and slid the king into position. I kept the queen in my hand, refusing to put it down, as I slid the ace next to the king.

Joanne stared at me. I stared back. Behind me, I could hear the crowd growing restless.

Finally, Joanne said, "No, the organization is not in any financial trouble." She said it clearly and firmly. Most importantly, she didn't twirl her hair.

I felt my whole body slump. I thought that I would at least be able to confirm a motive for Joanne. I put the queen down on the table.

Behind me the crowd cheered.

"A royal flush!" George squealed.

I looked across at Joanne. She didn't even bother to show me her hand, instead tossing the cards on the table with a scowl, conceding that I had won.

"Nice playing," Mr. Rainey said to me as I gathered my chips.

"That was really incredible, Nancy," Carla said. "I've been watching poker since I was five years old and I can count on one hand how many royal flushes I've seen."

Brett mumbled something under his breath, but I couldn't understand what he said. Even though I'd spent only a couple of hours with him, I knew that was the closest to any kind of congratulations he would give me.

"All right," Robert said. "We'll take a twenty-minute break before we head into the final stretch to see who will win the coveted trophy."

Bess and George ran over to me. Bess threw her arms around me.

"That was awesome!" George said. "Although I do have to admit that I'm a little jealous. I've never gotten a royal flush ever, and you play poker a handful of times and you get one."

"It was really impressive," Bess agreed.

"Thanks," I said.

"What's wrong?" George asked.

"Did something happen with the case?" Bess whispered.

I looked around. Joanne and Brett were still hovering by the table.

"I could really use some fresh air," I said, nodding toward the empty outer deck. Bess and George understood immediately.

We stepped outside. The air was cold, but it felt good.

"Poker is exhausting," I said, appreciating how the bracing air was waking me up.

"It really is," George said. "It takes a lot of concentration."

"Any new thoughts on the case?" Bess asked.

"Not really," I said. "I know there's something going on with both of them, but I can't prove that it has anything to do with the money. I'm starting to wonder if either of them is involved at all."

"Really?" George asked.

"Yeah," I said. "Well, at least not Joanne." I explained how I had worked out her tell and how she used it not just when she lied playing poker, but also when she lied in real life. "So I don't think she was lying when she said Kitty Kings wasn't in financial trouble," I said.

"As suspects they were good bets," Bess said. "They both had a motive and they both acted weird around the crash."

"I know, but if I've learned anything in the past hour, it's that you can't only take the safe bet. Sometimes you have to take a risk."

"It's true," George agreed. "You gather information about your fellow players and then you make your move."

Out of the corner of my eye something caught my

attention. I looked closer. "Catherine?" I said. "Is that you?"

Catherine stood up and came over to us. "Oh, hi," she said. "I was hoping you wouldn't notice me."

"Sorry," I replied.

"Are you okay?" Bess asked.

"Yeah. I was just missing my mom. She loves this river. She actually met my dad on a riverboat, so it's really tough that she's not here. I don't know if she'll ever get to see the river again." She was clearly fighting tears.

"That's really rough," I said. "Is there nothing they can do?"

"There's an experimental treatment for her cancer that's giving us some hope, but the insurance won't pay for it. I don't know what we're going to do. I just wish I could be with her tonight."

None of us knew what to say. After a moment, Catherine straightened up. "I see Margot pacing frantically inside." We turned and looked through the window. She was right; Margot did seem very agitated. "She's probably wondering where I am," Catherine continued. "I should go back in. Thanks for listening."

"Anytime," Bess said.

Catherine left us and we were quiet for a moment.

All of a sudden, a groaning noise emitted from the boat. It felt like we came to a grinding halt. We all took a step forward, temporarily thrown off balance by the change in speed.

"What's going on?" Bess asked.

I wasn't sure, until slowly the boat started turning around.

"We're headed back," I said. "I'm running out of time." It was hard to keep the dismay out of my voice.

"You can do this," Bess tried to reassure me.

"What if I can't solve it?" I said. "What if all those cats and dogs suffer because of me? And what if Catherine missed out on spending time with her mom for no reason?"

"That's not going to happen," Bess said firmly. "You are Nancy Drew!"

"She's right," George said. "You can solve anything you put your mind to."

I looked around, trying to come up with a new angle on the case. It really felt magical as we floated through the darkness, the lights from the banks twinkling. Watching all the people inside the brightly lit main room made it feel like we were in our own little floating world.

Through the window, I spotted Andy and Patrick together. They were both gesturing rapidly.

"Look," I said, pointing toward them.

"Are they fighting?" George asked.

"It certainly looks like it," Bess said.

Suddenly it hit me.

"Joanne said that Kitty Kings is doing fine financially," I said.

George and Bess looked back at me blankly.

"We assumed that they would steal the money in order to support their own organization," I said.

"Right," Bess said. "We thought they would try to hurt Margot's charity and help their own."

"Yeah," I said, "but what if it has nothing to do with their charity? What if they personally need the money?"

"Do you want to take another run at Joanne?" George asked.

"I think it's time to play a different card," I answered as I headed toward the door.

"Incorporating poker metaphors already," George commented. "You learn fast, grasshopper."

We went back into the main room and headed toward Patrick and Andy. Before we could get there, though, they separated, Patrick heading in one direction and Andy the other.

I hesitated for a moment, not sure who to follow.

"Which way?" George asked.

I stood paralyzed in the middle of the floor. It was like I could hear the clock ticking. I looked back and forth between Andy and Patrick. Patrick veered to the right and entered the men's room.

"Andy," I said. "Let's go."

We picked up the pace and headed toward Andy as

he made his way into the kitchen. He went through the door. I looked around and grabbed a tray filled with glasses that was sitting on a stand just outside the door. I heaved it onto my shoulder. It was heavier than it looked. The empty glasses swayed on top, and for a second I was terrified that they would tumble to the ground and shatter, but I managed to get the tray stabilized. Bess and George pushed the door open for me, and I walked into the restricted area before heading left into the kitchen.

The kitchen was a whirlwind of activity. Waiters were moving in and out, picking up full trays and returning empty ones. Cooks were working the line, prepping, cooking, and plating appetizer after appetizer. It was chaotic and orderly at the same time.

I spotted Andy in the corner, loading a tray with plates of chicken skewers. I put my tray of glasses down, and we made our way to him.

We'd gone only a few steps when all of a sudden a voice yelled out, "Hey! You can't be back here."

I turned to see a red-faced man who looked to be

in his forties and sported a chef's hat pointing at me with a spatula.

"I'm just—" I started, but the man didn't let me finish.

"I don't care. No guests in the kitchen." He crossed over to us, still brandishing his spatula. "No guests in the kitchen," he repeated as he herded us to the door.

He escorted us back into the restricted area and then returned to the kitchen.

Bess, George, and I stood for a moment, processing what had just happened.

"Now what are we going to do?" Bess asked.

"Do you want to try Patrick?"

"I gue—" I started to say, but trailed off when I spotted a doorway across the hall marked BREAK ROOM. I had missed it earlier. There was a narrow window cut into the door, which revealed a row of lockers against the wall.

"Lockers," I said, indicating the door.

"They're probably for the crew," Bess said. "A place for them to store their stuff while they work."

"And their money," I added.

We didn't say a word, just walked through the door. The room was cluttered with an old, ratty couch, a few tables, and even a sad, dead plant that looked like it hadn't been watered in several months. Coats and food wrappers were strewn about. Lockers lined the room's perimeter, covering the portholes. With only a dim ceiling light, the room felt dark and claustrophobic.

"Here's Andy's locker," George said, pointing to one in the corner that was labeled with his name. "But it's locked tightly." She tugged on the combination lock hanging from the handle.

"I know how to crack those," I said.

"You do?" George asked. "I thought I was the lock picker in this group."

"My dad bought a safe a long time ago in order to store his passport and some other important papers, but when he needed to get into it before a trip, he'd forgotten the combination. I spent the whole weekend learning how to crack it."

"Hey, I want to learn too!" Bess laughed.

"It's not that hard. You know when you spin a combination lock, you can kind of feel the lock click into place?" I asked.

Bess nodded.

"You can use that feeling to find the combination on any lock."

"Can you crack it in ten minutes?" George asked. "Because that's how much time there is until you have to get back to the game."

"I can crack it in two," I said, "but I need one of you to take notes."

"On it," Bess said, extracting a tiny notebook and a pen from her purse.

I leaned forward and tugged down gently on the lock, pulling on the shackle—the loop at the top that goes through the hole in the locker—so that the dial resisted as I tried to turn it. The lock made a grinding sound, so I slowly released the pressure on the shackle and kept spinning the dial clockwise. It still resisted, so I lightened the pressure a little more and spun the dial again. This time it resisted at only one spot.

"Okay," I said. "It's resisting between the eleven and the twelve, so we round up to twelve and add five."

"That's seventeen," George said.

"Seventeen is our first number. Bess, write that down."

"Okay," she said. "Why do you add five?"

"It's just a quirk of the lock that the first resistance point is always off. On these locks, which are the most common brand, it's off by five. Other brands it's by two, others three, and so forth."

I stretched my hand and got to work on finding the second number. I pulled down harder on the shackle again, and this time I spun the dial counterclockwise. It offered a lot of resistance, and after three turns, the dial wouldn't move at all anymore. It stuck at number twenty-three.

"Is that our second number?" George asked.

"It is," I said.

"Got it," Bess said. "We have seventeen, twenty-three."

"Okay," I said. "Here we go. Let's find this last number."

"And the money," George added.

"And the money," I agreed. "I'm going to say a bunch of numbers, Bess, I need you to write them all down."

I spun the dial clockwise a few times to reset the lock. Then, starting at zero, I turned it clockwise, pulling down on the lock as hard as I could. Every time the lock caught, I told Bess a number.

When I was done, I asked her to read them back.

"Four, sixteen, twenty-four, twenty-five, thirty-two."

"Hey," George said, "Four of those are multiples of four."

"And one's not," Bess said.

"The odd one out is our last number," I said, as I spun the dial clockwise again to reset it. "Okay. Read me back the numbers."

"Seventeen," Bess said. I turned the dial to seventeen.

"Twenty-three," she read out from her notes.

I went counterclockwise all the way to twenty-three.

"Twenty-five."

I turned it clockwise again, back around to twenty-five.

"Moment of truth," I said. I pulled down on the lock and the shackle gave way, giving us access to the locker.

"That was amazing," Bess said.

"Thanks," I said. "And now if you ever forget your locker combination, you know how to open it up. Okay, let's see if Andy has the money." I unhooked the lock and swung open the door. It was a generous locker. Andy could easily fit the money inside . . . but it was empty, except for his jacket and his phone.

None of us said anything, but we were all disappointed.

I picked up Andy's phone. "Joanne paid Andy to take her into the restricted area. Maybe they discussed the terms over e-mail."

"Are you sure about this?" George said. "Reading someone's e-mail is a big deal."

I hesitated. George was right. This was an invasion of Andy's privacy.

"He might have helped steal a hundred thousand dollars from charity," Bess countered. "I think it's worth reading the e-mail to find out one way or another."

George didn't look convinced, and I could understand why. Just because one person did something wrong didn't mean *I* should do something wrong trying to catch them. It was that old cliché that two wrongs don't make a right. I looked at my watch. I had only a little over an hour left; I was running out of options.

"How about this," I suggested. "I'll search the e-mail for Joanne's name, and I'll only look at e-mails from her. That way I'll only see messages that incriminate him."

George thought for a second and then nodded. "That seems like a fair compromise."

Luckily, his phone wasn't password protected, so I was able to open his e-mail app with no problem. I opened it and entered JOANNE into the search bar. Dozens of e-mails popped up.

"Not to pressure you," Bess said, "but you need to be back in the game in five minutes."

I skimmed through the most recent e-mails as fast as I could, trying to be mindful to ignore any that did not seem relevant to this case. Finally I landed on a promising one.

"Joanne isn't the culprit," I said.

"How do you know?" George asked.

I handed her the phone, and as she and Bess read the e-mail, I watched their eyes.

"Joanne and Patrick want to buy the *Delta Queen*!?" George squawked.

I nodded. "It makes sense. They paid Andy to take Joanne into the restricted area so they could see just how well the inner workings of the ship were holding up. Now they'll know exactly how much the boat is worth the minute it hits the market."

"So they can put their offer in while everyone else is still assessing the boat's value?" Bess clarified.

I nodded glumly. "The only suspect we have now is Brett."

"You always say that eliminating a suspect is just as important as discovering a new clue," George reminded me.

"I know," I said, "and that's true. I just don't feel

like we ever got a handle on who the suspects *are*. I think we're missing someone."

"Well, let's get back out onto the casino floor," Bess said.

"Yeah," George said. "We're lucky no one's caught us in here yet."

We shut the locker and headed back to the casino.

"The game starts up again in two minutes," George said, as we walked onto the main deck.

"It's still the only way I can get close enough to—"

Before I could finish my sentence, there was a scream from outside, followed by a splash.

George, Bess, and I looked at one another, alarmed.

"Woman overboard!" the PA system blared. "Woman overboard!"

❧

CHAPTER NINE

Locked Out

WE FOLLOWED THE CROWD OUT OF THE main room and to the deck outside. It seemed like the entire gala was there. Questions filtered their way through the crowd.

"Who fell in?"

"Is she okay?"

"How cold is that water, anyway?"

We pushed through to the railing, earning some dirty looks in the process, and leaned over to look into the river below.

"There," George said, pointing to a figure splashing in the water, frantically waving her arms.

"It's Catherine!" Bess exclaimed.

George and I looked closer.

"You're right," I said.

"Excuse me, coming through! Out of the way!" I heard Buddy yelling. I turned my head to see him charging toward us, clutching a life preserver that was attached to a rope. Carefully setting the life preserver down, he tied the rope to the railing.

"Hang on!" he yelled as he leaned back and heaved the life preserver over the side of the boat with a strained groan. It hit the water with a loud splash.

"Grab on to it and put it over your head, under your shoulders. When it's in position, give me a thumbs-up." He was yelling so that Catherine could hear him, but he didn't sound scared. He sounded like he knew exactly what to do.

I felt my heartbeat slow down a tad. Buddy was taking charge of the situation. Everything was going to be okay.

George, Bess, and I peered over the railing along with the entire crowd. Below us Catherine struggled to hang on to the life preserver. It seemed to keep slipping out of her grasp.

"What's happening?" Bess asked, her voice tense. "Why can't she grab it?"

"That water's probably thirty degrees," George said. "Hypothermia could already be setting in."

"Just grab it and put it over your head! You can do this!" Buddy hollered.

"Shouldn't someone jump in after her?" George asked.

"Not yet," Buddy explained. "She's conscious and she's following directions. I don't want to risk anyone else's life yet."

The wake of the boat kicked off a small wave. It washed over Catherine, who bobbed below the surface. We waited for her to come up, but she didn't. The water remained still and dark.

I looked over at Buddy. "Come up. Come up. Come up," he repeated to himself over and over under his breath, as if he were begging her to surface. I looked at his face. He no longer looked confident and in control; he looked terrified.

I felt my heart race and my breath quicken. If Buddy was scared, then I knew this was serious. Beside me George's face was frozen, as if she couldn't move until she knew Catherine was okay. Bess stared at the water.

I looked down. There was still no sign of Catherine. The life preserver bobbed on the water's surface.

A murmur made its way through the crowd as people realized that something was seriously wrong. My stomach felt like I had swallowed a stone.

"Now I'm going in," Buddy announced. He climbed up on the rail and was about to jump when all of a sudden there was a splash. Catherine burst through to the surface, gasping for air. She grabbed hold of the life preserver and slipped it over her head and under her shoulders, exactly as Buddy had instructed. Then she waved her hand above her head.

"She's giving the thumbs-up sign!" Bess said.

"Pull her up! Pull her up!" George shouted.

Buddy hopped down from the railing, grabbed the rope, and slowly towed Catherine to the boat. After he had pulled her up and over the railing, she collapsed onto the deck, breathing hard. She was shivering and her skin was shriveled and pale. A crew member rushed over with a blanket. Buddy took it from him and wrapped Catherine in it. It almost looked like he hugged her for a second, but it was fleeting. I briefly wondered if they knew each other.

Mrs. Marvin rushed over and enveloped Bess in a hug, then hugged George and me.

"I'm so glad you girls are okay," she said. "When I heard someone had gone overboard, I was sure it was one of you because of the case."

Margot fought her way over to Catherine as well.

"What happened?" Margot asked.

"I don't know," Catherine said, rubbing her eyes and then tugging on her ear, as if getting the water out. "I realized I dropped my keys when I was out here earlier. I came out to look for them, and before I knew what was happening, someone pushed me over the side."

"You're sure someone pushed you?" I asked.

Catherine gave me a look like this was the dumbest question she had ever heard. "Of course I'm sure," she said.

"Did you get a look—" I started, but Buddy cut me off.

"We all have a lot of questions for Catherine," he said, "but we need to get her inside and warmed up before she gets hypothermia."

He helped Catherine up and ushered her inside, his arm around her protectively. Margot and Mrs. Marvin held back.

The excitement over, most of the crowd drifted back inside. Only a handful of people stayed out in the cold.

"Please tell me you know who did this," Margot said. Mrs. Marvin looked at me hopefully.

"Well," I said, "we know that Joanne and Patrick don't have anything to do with it."

"That's great," Margot said sarcastically. "I also

know I didn't do it. The point is to find out who *did* do it."

I knew she was under a lot of stress, but I wished she could be just a little more kind.

"Right now, Brett is our prime suspect," I said.

"Brett Garner, our guest of honor?" Margot hissed, gesturing toward him standing a few yards away. Even in the midst of a crisis, he still had his backpack. There was definitely something important in there.

I nodded.

"Do you have any proof?" Mrs. Marvin asked.

"Not yet," I said, "but Catherine may have seen more than she thinks she did."

"You think the thief was trying to get her out of the way?" George asked.

"It's possible," I replied. "We need her to go over everything she saw before the money went missing. Something she didn't think was important could actually be a clue."

"Well, I can tell you for a fact that that Brett Garner didn't push Catherine over the side of the boat," Margot said. "I saw him sitting at the table when Catherine went overboard. Who else?"

"Um, well—"

"Great," Margot said, walking away from me mid-sentence. "My money gets stolen, my employee's life is endangered, and my crack detective hasn't got a clue." The door slammed behind her.

My friends looked at me sympathetically.

"Don't take it personally," Mrs. Marvin said. "Margot is a genius when it comes to cats and dogs, but she's not as good with people. I have faith in you."

"Thanks," I said, but I couldn't help feeling like I was letting Mrs. Marvin down.

"I'm going to find out how Catherine is doing," Mrs. Marvin said.

"You guys should, too," I said to George and Bess, pulling myself together. "If she feels up to answering questions, see if she remembers anything."

"Sure," Bess agreed. "What are you going to do?"

"I'll take a look out here and see if there are any clues."

Bess, George, and Mrs. Marvin went back inside. I looked across the river as a lighthouse blinked on the shoreline.

I didn't know exactly where Catherine went over the railing, so I headed toward the bow of the boat. If I was lucky, maybe in the exertion of pushing Catherine over, the culprit had dropped something.

I thought the deck was empty, so I jumped when a voice spoke out.

"You coming back to the game?"

I looked up to see Brett standing in front of me. For the first time all evening, he wasn't wearing his sunglasses. With his big round eyes, he looked significantly less intimidating than he did with his shades on.

"You coming back into the game?" Brett repeated, and I realized I hadn't answered.

"In a minute," I said.

"Well, don't take too long," Brett said. "Or we'll have to start without you."

"I know," I said.

He walked away, and I was left shaking my head.

He was definitely an odd guy. I hoped that after all this George would find a different favorite poker player.

I continued my search of the deck. My dad had taught me that when police conduct searches, they break the area into a grid to make sure every section is searched. I tried to follow the same technique. I found what I assumed were Catherine's keys (there was a key chain that said CATHERINE attached to them) and some scattered cocktail napkins people must have dropped in the commotion, but nothing that pointed toward the culprit.

I stuck the keys in my purse, reminding myself to give them back to Catherine when I saw her. I was disappointed that I hadn't found anything more.

I headed back toward the door to rejoin my game. But when I pulled on the handle, it didn't move. I tried again, harder, but still nothing.

The door was locked!

CHAPTER TEN

~

A Daring Journey

I KNOCKED ON THE DOOR, BUT WITH THE music blaring, no one could hear me. I knocked louder, but it was no use. No one even glanced toward the door.

I pulled out my phone, hoping that maybe the lack of cell service George had observed earlier was temporary, but I was out of luck there, too. My screen showed no bars.

Through the windows, I could see that people were going in and out of doors on the other side of the boat. If I could get over there, I could get back inside, but how to get there?

I walked to the back of the boat. The wall of the engine room abutted the end of the boat, separating the deck I was on from the one on the other side. But when I looked more closely, I noticed a narrow ledge that ran against the wall; I could definitely slide myself across that to get to the other side. The only problem was that directly beneath it the paddle wheel churned, propelling the boat forward. If I fell, I would almost certainly hit my head on one of the slats. I could get seriously hurt, or worse.

I paused. There were good risks and there were bad risks. Bess and George would notice I was missing soon enough and come looking for me. But after how long? I knew they would be thorough with Catherine, which could keep them occupied for a while. I was already shivering, and I needed to get back to the table before I was out of the game. If I was going to try to make my way across the ledge, I needed to do it before I got any colder.

Not to mention our culprit was getting more and more dangerous. Pushing Catherine off the side of the boat was serious. Who knew what he or she would do next?

I looked at the ledge again. It was narrow and it was a long way down to the river, but I couldn't think of a better move.

I spied the life preserver Buddy had thrown to Catherine, sitting in the middle of the deck. Buddy had tossed it aside once Catherine was back onboard. I picked it up, surprised by how light it was. It seemed like Buddy had really put his back into throwing it over the side of the boat, so I had imagined it to be much heavier, but it only weighed a pound or two.

I slipped it over my head before noticing that there was a large rip in the side of it. This wouldn't do me any good. Sighing, I put it back on the ground. A vision of myself plunging into the dark, cold water flooded my head, but I shook it off. I could do this.

I climbed onto the ledge until I was sitting on it facing the river. As soon as I did, a cold wind blasted my face. I realized that I had been protected from the wind on my side of the boat. It was hard to keep my eyes open. My hands struggled to keep a tight grip around the ledge, which was narrower than I had realized. When I looked across, I saw that it was about forty feet to the other side. Time to get moving.

I extended my right foot to the side and hooked it to a steel bar below me, using the leverage to pulley myself along the railing. When I looked back I realized I'd gone about six inches. Only eighty more moves like that and I'd be across. I repeated the motion again and again. After a while, it was like my body was there, but my mind was elsewhere. All I was focused on was sliding six inches at a time. I looked down and realized I had made it halfway across. Despite the conditions, I found myself smiling. My hands were numb, and my feet ached, but I was doing it!

I reached my foot over again and started to slide, but this time it slipped and I lurched off the ledge, my entire right side falling forward. I barely caught myself with my left hand. My feet dangled below me, inches above the slats of the paddle wheel. I could hear the water churning below as spray from the river hit my legs.

I thrashed my feet, desperate to find a foothold to lift me back onto the railing, but my feet weren't finding anything. I tried to grab the railing with my right arm, but I couldn't reach. My left arm was getting tired, and the pain in my shoulder was growing more acute. I wasn't sure how much longer I would be able to hold on.

The churning of the paddle wheel felt like it was getting louder. Of course it was only my imagination, but it felt like the paddle was creating a vacuum that was pulling on my feet, trying to suck me into its slats. My mind went blank as adrenaline poured through me. I didn't know what to do.

Suddenly my right foot caught on something. I tentatively pushed my weight on it. It was a narrow ledge of some kind. I couldn't see what it was, but it felt strong enough to hold my weight. Very slowly, I pushed down and extended my knee. My foothold was tenuous. I was aware that any second I could go tumbling again, and this time I had no faith that my left arm would be able to hold my weight. I got high enough to swing my right arm back onto the ledge. Using both arms and the foot-hold, I was able to haul myself back onto the ledge.

I didn't even stop to collect myself. I wanted off this ledge and both feet firmly planted on a deck as soon as possible.

It took close to ten more minutes, but I made it to the other side. I collapsed to the ground, grateful to have both feet under me. It wasn't quite solid ground, but I would take it.

After a moment of catching my breath, I headed back into the main deck. Bess and George spotted me immediately and rushed over. Mrs. Marvin was right behind them.

"Nancy!" Bess said. "Are you okay?"

"We've been looking all over you," George added.

I opened my mouth to explain what had happened, but all that came out was a raspy croak.

"Nancy, you need water," Mrs. Marvin exclaimed, rushing off to get me some.

When she came back, I drank it all down with one gulp.

"Thanks," I said. "I didn't realize how thirsty I was."

I quickly explained what had happened. Bess, George, and Mrs. Marvin were horrified.

"I don't want you investigating this incident anymore," Mrs. Marvin said.

"I think my mom's right." Bess nodded. "It's too dangerous."

"I agree," George said. "This thief has already pushed one person overboard. They must know that you're investigating and now they're going after you."

I shook my head. "We're still half an hour away from docking, and the thief clearly knows that I'm onto them. The safest thing for me to do is solve this case once and for all. Beside, I can't let him get away with it."

"Him?" Bess asked. "Do you know who it is?"

I nodded, looking at George. "I'm sorry, but I'm certain it's Brett."

"But we know he didn't push Catherine," George said.

"He might have a partner, but I know he's the one

who locked me out there. He was the last person to leave."

George and Bess exchanged a look. "I don't know if that's enough evidence for Margot to go to the police with."

"I know Margot," Mrs. Marvin said. "She's going to want more concrete proof than that before she confronts her guest of honor."

I looked across the room at the final table. It looked like Joanne and Mr. Rainey had busted out since I had been gone; just Carla and Brett were left. Brett's backpack was still under his chair. The pile of chips in front of Brett was almost twice as big as Carla's. It seemed like he'd gone on a run and had won most of Joanne and Mr. Rainey's chips. My pile had been significantly depleted. George wasn't kidding when she'd said that antes could bleed you dry.

"Then let's get some proof," I said.

I could feel the entire room's eyes on me as I marched over to the table, with Bess, George, and Mrs. Marvin trailing behind me. I knew I looked like a wreck. As I passed under the rope, Brett looked up at me. I couldn't see behind his sunglasses, but I imagined the expression on his face was smug.

"Oh, hey, Nancy," he said. "I wasn't sure you were going to make it back. I thought maybe you got detained."

I didn't say anything; I just made a beeline for his backpack. Many times your job as a detective is getting information without anyone realizing what you're doing. You have to be discreet. You have to charm. You have to coerce. You have to finagle. But often there's no time for subtlety; you have to get the information using whatever means necessary.

Brett looked at me, confused. He didn't understand why I wasn't sitting down in my seat. Only as I came right behind his chair did he realize what was happening, but it was too late. I already had my hand on the bag, and I yanked it out of his reach.

"Hey!" he yelled. "You can't look in there!"

Margot had noticed the commotion and joined the group.

"Nancy, what are you doing?" she asked. "This is highly inappropriate."

But I ignored both of them. Bess and George formed a protective wall around me so Brett couldn't grab the backpack back.

I yanked the zipper open and plunged my hand into the bag.

CHAPTER ELEVEN

❧

Confession

MY HAND CLOSED AROUND SOMETHING square. I could feel other similar items in the bag. They almost felt like stacks of money. But when I pulled one out, I realized it was a pack of cards.

I reached into the bag again and pulled out another pack of cards. And another.

Brett had a look of terror on his face. I stared at the cards, confused. This wasn't what I was expecting to find.

"Brett, I am so sorry," Margot said. "I will deal with

Nancy. She never should have violated your privacy like that."

George came up behind me. "Let me look at those," she said. I handed her a pack and she quickly flipped through it. Her face fell.

"These cards are marked," she said quietly.

Margot stopped talking to Brett and turned to George. "Are you absolutely sure?"

George nodded grimly.

"What does that mean?" Bess asked.

"I'll show you," George said. "Hang on a second." She walked over to a nearby table and picked up another deck of cards. She spread that deck and one of Brett's decks out on the table, facedown. "Can you see the difference?"

They were both red with cherubic figures in the center and an intricate design around the sides involving swirls and abstract flowers.

"They both look the same to me," Bess said.

"Look harder," George said.

Bess and I peered more closely. Suddenly I saw

it! "On these cards," I said, indicating the pack from Brett's bag, "some of the leaves around the edges are filled in. But on this other deck none of them are." It was subtle, but once I saw it, I couldn't unsee it.

"I see it too," Bess said.

"Me too," Mrs. Marvin added.

Margot shook her head furiously. "I can't believe you," she said to Brett.

"It's not what you think," Brett said meekly, but Margot clearly didn't believe him.

"But how does that help?" I asked.

"Watch this," George said. Her hands flying, she grabbed several cards from Brett's spread-out deck and arranged them on the table.

"What do you notice now?"

"The leaf that's colored in is in a different place on each card," Bess said.

"It almost looks like a clock the way it moves around the cards," I noticed.

"Yep," George said. "And that clock tells you what card it is. For example, this one," she said, pointing to a card where the leaf colored in was directly in the middle at the top, "is an ace." She held the card up, so only Bess and I could see it. "Am I right?"

She was. "It's an ace of spades," I confirmed.

"And this one," she said, holding up a card that was marked at the nine o'clock position, "is a ten." Again she was right.

"But this one isn't marked," I noted.

"That's the king. This is a really old trick that card cheats have been using for at least a hundred years," George explained.

"So you knew what cards all of us were holding in every hand!" I said. "You weren't winning by skill at all."

Brett nodded meekly.

"How did you switch the decks?" Margot asked indignantly.

"Did you cause Andy and Joanne to crash into each other to get the real cards wet, so you could make the switch?" I asked as the realization hit me.

Brett just nodded again. "I threw a salt shaker on the ground right as Andy was walking by."

I shook my head in disbelief.

"I know it was wrong, but what was the harm?" Brett protested.

"What's the harm!?" Margot squawked. "You ruined the integrity of my event!"

"You were cheating," Mrs. Marvin said sternly.

"Yeah, but people still got to play with me," Brett argued. "Pet Crusaders still made money. Who cares if I won for real or by cheating?"

George, Bess, and I were all speechless. He was right, I supposed, in that no actual harm had been done, but it still felt wrong. People had paid to play an honest game against him, to test their skill against a true professional player, and they had been cheated of that experience.

"That's not the point," Mrs. Marvin said to Brett. "And you know that. You let down a lot of people who were looking forward to meeting you."

"If you think we will still be paying you an appearance fee, you have another think coming," Margot said.

Brett shook his head. "I really need that money!"

"Well, you should have thought about that before you treated my event with disrespect," Margot said. "I can't even look at you right now," she added as she stormed off.

"Donating that fee to this organization is the least you can do," Mrs. Marvin said before she turned and followed Margot.

"Have you been pulling this stunt your whole career?" Bess asked Brett.

"What? No!" Brett protested. "I won my World Series of Poker bracelets fair and square."

Bess looked at him skeptically. One thing I've learned as a detective is that people tend to make the same mistakes over and over. When you're looking for a culprit, the first person you want to look for is someone who has done something similar before.

"I believe him," George said, noting the disbelief on our faces. "Professional poker players would have caught this really quickly. Not to mention the millions of fans watching on TV. He never would have gotten away with this in a professional tournament."

"I saw the letter," I admitted. "I know you're losing your sponsorship, but I don't understand how winning a charity tournament against amateurs helps you."

"I'm being considered by another sponsor, but if I lost a tournament to amateurs, they'd never take me on. They'd really think I was washed up."

"But poker is half luck," George pointed out. "No one can hold losing one tournament against you."

"They can when you haven't won a tournament in two years," Brett said. "I couldn't risk having more bad luck. The stakes are too high for me. I've been playing poker professionally since I was twenty-one years old. Beside waiting tables in college, I've never had another job. If I don't get another sponsor, I don't know what I will do with my life."

"But what about locking me outside without a coat?" I asked. "Why did you do that?"

"I'm sorry about that," Brett said. "But I thought you were onto me."

"I almost fell into the river!" I exclaimed.

"I was going to let you back in. I just wanted to win the tournament first."

I shook my head. Part of me felt sorry for him. Maybe if he had just cheated during the game I could have forgiven him, but he'd also put my life at risk. His career and ego did not make that okay.

"Let's go," I said to George and Bess. "We have work to do."

My friends and I made our way to an empty table all the way in the corner and slumped into our seats.

"He was one of my heroes," George said. "I can't believe that someone I looked up to would do something like that."

"At least you don't have to feel bad that you didn't get to play against him," Bess said.

"That's true," George said.

Bess turned to me. "How about you, Nancy? How are you doing?"

"We have nothing," I said. "We solved a case, but it was the wrong one."

"We have *something*," Bess said.

"From the start, we operated on the assumption that the crash was a distraction so the thief could get into the safe," I said. "But now we know that the crash was a distraction so that Brett could switch the cards. We don't even know when the money was stolen."

"Well," Bess said, "we know it was stolen within the first half hour of the gala, because that's when Catherine and Margot discovered it was missing."

"What did Catherine say when you talked to her?" I asked.

"She didn't say much," George said.

"She was still really shaken up from the fall," Bess explained.

"She said she didn't remember anything unusual happening either before the money was stolen or when she was out on the deck," George said.

"We tried to ask her a few questions, but Buddy made us leave," Bess said. "He was very protective of her."

"Sorry, Nancy. I know we didn't get the information you were hoping for," George apologized.

"It's okay," I said. "I can't believe I thought this case was going to be easy."

"It makes sense," said George. "How often do you do have all your suspects trapped in one place?"

We sat in silence. I racked my brain, trying to come up with another angle, to find the piece that I had missed.

"Let's go through all the clues again," I said. "From the beginning. Let's cross out everything that was due to Joanne and Patrick evaluating the boat and everything that was due to Brett switching the decks."

George pulled out her phone. "Okay, I'll take notes."

"First we wondered why Joanne and Patrick were here, helping Margot's organization," Bess said.

"Right, but now we know it was just so they would have access to the *Delta Queen*," I said.

"There was the crash between Joanne and Andy," George said.

"But Brett admitted that he orchestrated that as an excuse to switch the decks," Bess said.

"I was locked out," I said.

"That was also Brett," George pointed out.

"Catherine was thrown overboard," Bess added.

I thought for a second. There was something nagging at me. But before I could think of it, the horn blared.

"Attention, everyone," Buddy announced over the PA system. "We will be docking in five minutes. Please take this time to gather your belongings. We will be exiting off the stern side. It has been a pleasure to have you onboard."

I felt like I had been punched in the stomach. I knew solving a case in three hours would be a challenge, but I'd never thought I would completely fail. I didn't have a single lead.

"Come on," I said to Bess and George. "Let's find Margot and tell her she should call the police."

CHAPTER TWELVE

~

We're Gonna Need a Smaller Boat

THE PASSENGERS WERE GONE. I HAD WATCHED them stream off the boat, studying each one, hoping I would see something that would make it all fall into place, but I didn't notice anything out of the ordinary. I even kept a lookout for large bags so I could at least tell the police where to start, but I didn't see anything bigger than a briefcase.

Bess, George, and I were seated around the final table with Buddy, Margot, Catherine, and Mrs.

Marvin, waiting for the police to show up. Around us Andy and the other waiters cleaned up. There was a sad silence among all of us. In past years, this was when Mrs. Marvin, Margot, and the other organizers had celebrated a job well done. They would toast one another and make a big show of counting the money they'd earned. It was usually my favorite part of the evening. This year, there was no toast, no celebrating, and no one seemed relaxed. Everyone just wanted to go home.

"It's not all lost," Mrs. Marvin said to Margot. "The police could find the money. They'll monitor the financial activity of all our guests, and if someone makes an unusually large purchase, they'll investigate."

Margot shrugged. "I don't think so. Whoever did this is smart. They broke into a safe in the middle of a crowded boat, they hid the money onboard, and they got it off while we had a detective on the case. I don't think they're going to buy a fancy car tomorrow. They'll sit on the money and wait for a long enough time that no one will connect the expenditure to the theft, or they'll spend it slowly, never attracting attention. Either way that money is gone."

All the rage and fire that had been coursing through her the whole evening was gone. She reminded me of a deflated balloon.

She paused for a moment. Then she stood up. "I need some air. The police said they'd be here in ten minutes."

We watched her leave. As intense and difficult as she was, it was harder to see her like this. She didn't seem like the same person I had met three hours earlier. I couldn't help but feel a twinge of guilt. I wish I could have solved the case in time. Bess, always observant, noticed the look on my face.

"This isn't your fault," she whispered. "*You* didn't steal the money."

"I know," I said, "but I said I could find it and I didn't."

"You tried your best," Bess continued. "You aren't perfect." I knew Bess was right, but I still felt terrible. I hated letting people down.

I looked over at Catherine, who was wrapped in a blanket. I realized that there was still one angle of this investigation I hadn't fully explored. I set my jaw. There were still ten minutes before I had to turn this case over to the police.

"So, Catherine, now that you're warmed up, can you tell me more about what happened when you got pushed off the boat?"

Catherine looked up at me, surprised. "I really don't remember much," she said, rubbing her neck.

"Anything at all could be helpful," I prodded.

"Sorry. It all happened so fast," she said, quickly.

I studied her closely. I didn't believe her. I was sure she remembered something about the person who pushed her over.

"Even a sound or a smell could help narrow down the suspects," I insisted.

Catherine sighed, then looked at me directly. "I'm telling you," she said, rubbing her neck again, "I don't remember anything. Between the sound of the paddle wheel and the wind, I didn't even realize someone was out there before I felt hands on my back. The next thing I knew I was falling over the side of the boat."

All of a sudden it hit me. She was lying. Rubbing her neck was her tell. If I was right, it meant she was lying about everything she said happened on that deck. But why would she lie?

I felt my phone buzz, pulling me out of my reverie. I took it out to see a group text from Bess to George and me. Our cell service must have come back when we docked.

"I know that look," it read. "What have you figured out?"

"I need to go to the restroom," I announced.

George and Bess stood up too. "We'll go with you," Bess said.

Mrs. Marvin gave us a small nod. She could tell that we had made a break in the case.

We speed-walked across the boat to the restroom. Once we were inside, Bess locked the door and George spun toward me.

"What have you got, Nancy?" George asked.

I explained how I thought that Catherine rubbing her neck was a tell, that she was lying about not knowing anything about who pushed her off the boat.

"But why would she lie?" George asked.

"I don't know," I said. "Maybe she's protecting whoever it was."

"Yeah," George said, "but that person put her life in danger. Why would she stay loyal to them?"

I shrugged. "People are complicated. Maybe it's someone she's close to, like her best friend or her cousin."

"I don't get it," George complained. "Bess, if you pushed me off a boat, I would tell Nancy in a heartbeat."

"I doubt it," Bess said. "What if you knew that I needed the money for something really important?"

"Wait," I interrupted them before this disagreement spun out of control. "Her mom. She said there's a treatment that the insurance company won't pay for. So maybe Catherine needed the money to pay for her mom's hospital bills," I suggested. "She doesn't have a boat to sell like Buddy does. Plus, think about it," I continued. "We assumed the money was stolen from the safe, but Catherine is the one who handed the box of money to Margot to put into the safe. Do we even know that the money was in the box?"

"That's true," George said. "Catherine encouraged us to question all the guests."

"Do you think Catherine would betray Margot like that?" Bess asked. "She's worked for her for a long time."

"I don't know," I said, "but Margot wasn't particularly nice to her. She demanded that Catherine be here even though her mom was in the hospital. Maybe Catherine was tired of being treated badly."

"But if Catherine stole the money, who pushed her off the boat?" Bess asked.

"Maybe no one did," I said. "Maybe she jumped."

"Why would she do that?" George asked.

"To take any suspicion off her," I said. "And it worked. We've been thinking of her as a victim, not a suspect."

Bess and George nodded. I could see that they were toying with the idea of Catherine as the culprit.

"So if Catherine stole the money . . . ," I started.

"Then it's still on the boat!" Bess and George finished.

"We have to find it," I said.

George and Bess and I marched out of the bathroom on a mission.

"We should search around the check-in desk first," I said, "since that's where Catherine was stationed. Maybe she didn't move it far."

We headed toward the front of the boat, toward the check-in desk and office located right outside the main room, but before we could start looking, we were greeted by Margot leading two River Heights police officers onboard.

"Nancy!" I looked up to see that it was Officer Parker, a friend of my dad's. "If you're on the case, what am I doing here?"

"Unfortunately," Margot said, "Nancy was not able to solve this matter for us."

Officer Parker looked at me, surprised. He turned to his partner, whose uniform said ANG on it. "Nancy has a better solve rate than most of the detectives in our department," he said.

Officer Ang nodded. "So I've heard."

"Well, actually," I said, "I do have a new theory."

"Hit me with it," Officer Parker said.

I looked around, making sure that Catherine was still in the main room with Buddy and Mrs. Marvin, and then leaned in and explained how I thought the money was still on the boat and why.

"I can't believe Catherine would do that to me," Margot said.

Officer Parker nodded. "Well, we'll take a look for sure," he said. "You girls go into the main room with the others."

I started to tell him that I wanted to help too, but he cut me off before I could say anything. "It's protocol, Nancy," he said. "You know that. I can't let you help."

I sighed, disappointed, but we dutifully headed back to the main deck. If Officer Parker and Officer

Ang did find the money, I would know that I'd helped, but it wouldn't be as satisfying as finding it myself.

We sat down with Catherine, Buddy, and Mrs. Marvin. I could hear the officers moving tables, opening cabinets, and pushing aside chairs in the check-in area. Across from me, Buddy shifted uncomfortably.

"They'd better not break anything," he muttered.

The chaos continued next to us. I kept waiting to hear a triumphant shout that they'd found the money, but there was nothing; just the sounds of doors opening and closing. I started to get worried. There weren't that many places that the money would be hidden. Margot shifted her glare between me and Catherine. I couldn't tell whether she wanted me to be right. If I was right, she'd have her money back, but it would also mean she'd been betrayed by her most trusted employee. Even Mrs. Marvin shot me a worried glance.

There was a loud noise from the check-out desk.

"Seriously," Buddy grumbled. "I need this boat to be in peak condition. My mom's medical bills aren't going to pay for themselves."

My head shot up, a million thoughts flying through my brain. I looked between Catherine and Buddy as the pieces clicked together for the first time. They'd both said their mom was in the hospital. Catherine said her mom had met her dad on a riverboat. Buddy's stepdad had worked on a riverboat.

"You're half siblings," I blurted out. "You stole the money together."

"That's absurd," Buddy said.

"No, it's not," George said, holding up her phone. "I just found a wedding announcement for a Violet Gibson marrying a man named Frank Lewis, and it says here that Violet has a son named William 'Buddy' Gibson from a previous marriage."

"Okay, fine," Catherine said. "He's my half brother. That doesn't mean we stole the money."

Officers Parker and Ang entered the room.

"Sorry, Nancy," Officer Parker said. "We looked everywhere. No sign of the money."

"See," Buddy said. "We're not the thieves. The money's not on the boat."

I looked at him, my mind racing. Where could the money be? I was so close to solving this case, I could taste it, but it still felt so far.

My phone buzzed in my purse. I reached in to grab it, and my hand closed around something unfamiliar. I looked inside and realized it was the set of keys I'd found on the deck earlier. Beside the key chain with Catherine's name on it, I saw a second key chain I hadn't noticed before. It was for DEEP SEA ADVENTURES. It took a second for me to remember why that name sounded familiar: It was the logo on the oxygen tank I had seen in the restricted area!

Suddenly I knew. "You threw it overboard!" I said.

"They did what?" Margot shrieked.

I nodded. "The money was inside the life preserver that Buddy threw to Catherine. She took it out before she came back onboard."

"That's why she kept going under the water before she got herself into the life preserver," Bess said.

I nodded again. "And that's why the life preserver was so light when I picked it up, even though it looked so heavy when Buddy threw it over. And it explains the big rip in the side of the life preserver."

"Well, if that's true, how are we supposed find the money now?" asked Margot.

I indicated the watch Catherine was wearing, the one she and George had geeked out about earlier. "I'm pretty sure she logged the GPS coordinates where she dropped the money on her watch," I said. "There's scuba gear belowdecks. They were going to retrieve the money sometime later, once the coast was clear."

Officer Parker stepped forward. "Ma'am, I'm going to need to see the watch."

Catherine hesitated for a moment, but then she grudgingly handed it over. Officer Parker looked at the watch hopelessly for a few seconds before handing it to George.

"I don't know how to work this thing," he said. "Can you figure it out?"

George took the watch and hit a couple of buttons. We all watched as she manipulated the screen. No one said anything. There was a nervous energy floating through the air. My heart was racing.

"Found it," she said finally. "Right there. Those are coordinates that have been saved. I'm not an expert, but they seem close to where she went over." She handed the watch back to Officer Parker.

Margot turned on Catherine. "Please tell me this is all a big misunderstanding."

Catherine hesitated for a second, but then it came bursting out of her, as if she had been holding it in for hours, if not longer. "You raised all this money for your precious cats and dogs," she hissed defiantly, "but when I told you my mother was sick and asked for a raise, you said you couldn't afford it."

"It would have meant less money for the animals," Margot said, uncomprehendingly.

Catherine let out a frustrated sigh. "But what about me? What about my mother's life? Why don't we matter? And then when Buddy started talking about selling the *Delta Queen*, this boat he had wanted for so long, I knew I needed to do something. If we were successful in stealing the money, then he could take the *Delta Queen* off the market."

Mrs. Marvin put a sympathetic arm around Catherine. "I understand what you were going through, but this wasn't the way."

"Then what was the way?" Catherine asked. Even Mrs. Marvin didn't have an answer for that.

Officer Parker shook his head, then reached for his radio.

"We're gonna need a diver out at the dock," he said.

Half an hour later, George, Bess, and I were sitting in a motorboat with Officer Parker and Madison Jones, the police department's diver, racing down the river, retracing our route from earlier. This was an entirely different experience from our leisurely trip this evening. We were covering the same ground we had on the *Delta Queen* in about one-fourth the time. The sound of the engine was too loud for conversation.

As we pulled in front of the lighthouse, Officer Parker cut the motor.

"I think we're almost there," he said.

George consulted the watch. "Yeah," she agreed. "Just a few yards that way."

Officer Parker went where she directed.

"Here?" he asked.

George nodded.

"All right, Madison," Officer Parker said to the diver. "Time to do your thing."

"On it," Madison said, as she pulled the hood of her wet suit over her head and strapped on a weight belt and oxygen tanks. She made sure that all her equipment was working, then put on her face mask and flippers and secured her powerful flashlight.

"All set," she said. She moved to the edge of the boat, put her mouthpiece in, and dropped into the water with a small splash. We watched the ripples she created disappear. It was odd to know that she was swimming around in the river and there was no evidence of her on the surface.

"What if the current moved the money downstream?" George asked. "We might have no idea where it ended up."

"I think it'll be okay," I said. "Buddy and Catherine really thought this through. I bet they put weights in the bag to make sure it went straight down."

"You're right," George said. "I'm just nervous. I really want Pet Crusaders to get that money."

"I do too," Bess said. "But if it was really to pay for their mom's hospital bills, I understand why they did it."

"That's true," I said. Often capturing a culprit feels double-edged, and this case was no exception. On the one hand, it felt good to nab someone who had done wrong, but on the other hand, many people have good reasons for doing bad things. I didn't agree with what Buddy and Catherine had done, but I understood why they had done it. If my dad had been in the hospital and needed surgery, I'd do everything in my power to make sure he had it.

We were all quietly waiting for Madison to surface with the money. It felt like we had been there for hours, but when I checked my watch, it had been only twenty minutes. It was weird how time worked. Earlier in the evening an hour felt like a second and now every second felt like an hour.

Finally there was a splash, and a garbage bag edged its way over the side of the boat with a *thunk*. We all jerked back in surprise. The boat rocked precipitously. Shortly thereafter, Madison pulled herself into the boat, panting.

"That was really heavy," she said.

I looked at Officer Parker, who gave me a nod. "It's your case, Nancy. Go ahead and take a look."

I leaned forward and worked open the knot. The bag was ice cold and covered with dirt and other detritus from the river. My hands quickly grew numb, but I kept working. I wasn't going to be satisfied until I saw the money with my own eyes.

At long last, the knot came free, and I quickly opened the bag. All of us leaned forward. I closed my eyes, unexpectedly nervous. When I opened them, I was greeted with the sight of piles of cash. A wave of relief spread over me. I felt my shoulders unclench. I hadn't realized how nervous I had been that Madison wouldn't find the money.

"You did it, Nancy," Bess said, putting her arm around me. "You solved a case in record time."

"Thanks," I said. "I couldn't have done it without you guys."

"We're a good team," George agreed.

"Let's get this money back to Margot," I said.

Officer Parker nodded and started up the engine. I clung to the bag of money the entire way back to the dock.

Margot and Mrs. Marvin were waiting for us. When Margot saw the bag in my hand and the grins on our faces, she ran toward us. She checked the bag and threw her arms around me in a deep, appreciative hug. I was caught off guard—Margot hadn't struck me as a hugger—but I put my arms around her in return. Mrs. Marvin gave me a grateful smile.

"Thank you so much," Margot said, her head buried in my shoulder. "I can't tell you how much I appreciate all your help. I'm sorry I wasn't nicer to you."

"It's okay," I said. "You give so much to the animals, you don't have a lot left over for people."

"I'm going to change that," Margot said. I pulled

back and looked her in the eyes. There were no tics: no rubbing of her cheek, no pulling on her hair, no shifting of her mouth. I believed her.

Officer Ang came off the boat, escorting Catherine and Buddy to the police car. There was a tense moment as Margot and Mrs. Marvin exchanged looks with Buddy and Catherine, but to my surprise, Margot strode over to them.

"Can you hold on a second?" she asked Officer Ang.

Officer Ang nodded. "Just for a minute," he said.

Margot took a deep breath. "I'm going to pay the hospital bill," she said.

Buddy and Catherine looked at her in shock.

"You were right," she said to Catherine. "I should have valued you more. I should have given you that raise."

"Thank you," Catherine said. Buddy nodded, looking like he would cry if he spoke.

"We have to go," Officer Ang said.

The police car pulled away. Officer Parker and Madison headed off shortly afterward. Mrs. Marvin and Margot went to finish up on the boat, leaving Bess, George, and me alone in the parking lot.

"What do you want to do now?" George asked.

"Go home, turn off my alarm clock, and sleep for as long as I want," I said. "In fact, I don't want to look at a clock at all tomorrow."

"Fair enough," George said. "You definitely went all in tonight."

"And no more poker puns, either!" I said.

Bess and George laughed and we headed back to my car.

Dear Diary,

I COULDN'T BELIEVE I'D SOLVED A CASE so quickly. It was close, but in the end I was glad I had pushed myself. Sometimes you have to take yourself out of your comfort zone—take a gamble, as George would say—to grow as a person. I don't know if I'll ever solve a case that fast again, but I'm glad to know that I can.

New mystery. New suspense. New danger.

NANCY DREW DIARIES™

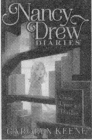

BY CAROLYN KEENE

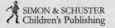

Did you LOVE reading this book?

Visit the Whyville...

Where you can:

- Discover great books!
- Meet new friends!
- Read exclusive sneak peeks and more!

Log on to visit now!
bookhive.whyville.net